SWEET NINETEEN

A Novel

ANTHONY MCDONALD

Anchor Mill Publishing

Sweet Nineteen

Anchor Mill Publishing

4/04 Anchor Mill

7 Thread Street

Paisley PA1 1JR

SCOTLAND

anchormillpublishing@gmail.com

Cover image: Detail from *The Sunbathers*; Henry Scott Tuke

Anthony McDonald

For Charles

Sweet Nineteen

ONE

It began on the bus. Promisingly or unpromisingly, with a morning hard-on. Mine. There was nothing unusual about it. It was eight in the morning. I was on my way to college. I was nineteen. It happened every morning. There was nothing that could be done about it. I had to conceal it as best I could from my neighbour, who was usually the same person, a middle-aged lady school teacher. She was very nice, actually, and we sometimes made a little small-talk during the five mile journey.

But this morning as I swung myself into my usual seat I found the window seat next to mine occupied, unexpectedly, by someone different. A boy of my age with thick black hair and headphones on. He didn't acknowledge my arrival in any way. I plonked myself down next to him. By the time we'd bumped along the first of those five miles through the Kentish apple orchards I found the usual thing stirring between my legs. But sitting next to a pleasing looking boy of my own age I felt less bothered than usual about needing to conceal the ridge that was building in the angle of my jeans.

Instead I glanced down casually at the equivalent bit of my new neighbour. And was stirred as well as startled to see that he was in the same state.

I looked across at his profile. He didn't look across at me. He was still listening to whatever was coming through his headphones – kerchugh, kerchugh, kerchugh was all I got of it – and he seemed unaware of me, even of the fact that I was there next to him. He certainly hadn't clocked the hard-on in my pants, and was perhaps unaware of the one in his own. Not that any of that bothered me. I was quite happy simply to observe his face from the side for a moment, and it was better to do that without his knowing.

He had very full lips. That was the first thing I noticed. Really nice ones, with a good colour that was almost as bright as raspberries. And while reaching into the fruit bowl for similes I may as well mention that his cheeks had the rounded look and healthy colour that together give rise to comparison with apples. His eyes... Well, you don't get a real impression from the side. It's only from the front, as a rule, that eyes are windows into the soul. But his were brown, I thought, or perhaps a very dark, almost coal-like, blue. Again difficult to tell from the side. Easier to see, and to appreciate, were his very long lush lashes. Which curled. The upper ones upwards and the lower, down, as if they sought to brush his ruddy cheeks.

I liked the look of what I saw. But therein a problem lay. I wasn't sure if I was supposed to like the looks of another boy so much. I had it on good authority that most boys my age preferred girls.

I liked the way girls looked, don't get me wrong. Or at least, some of them. (Nobody can like the appearance of every member of the opposite sex, or their own.) What was different in my case was that the looks of boys my age – again, not all of them, of course – elicited a response, part physical, part emotional, that was out of all proportion to anything I felt about even the loveliest female face or form I'd encountered... Up to now, at least.

There was an obvious conclusion to be drawn from this. That I was gay. I hadn't had a chance to put this to the test. Not properly. Though more of that anon. For the moment, this bouncing bus moment, I knew only that the presence of the boy beside me, his profile, his hormones, pheromones or whatever, to say nothing of the erection in his jeans, was giving me an almost indescribable feeling. It was as if a key were being turned somewhere deep inside me. To unlock something there? I had no idea. But I found myself suddenly, absurdly, feeling almost as happy as I could ever remember being. I discovered that this springy, grubby bus seat was the place I wanted most to be. I didn't want to be anywhere else in the world, and I didn't want this rapidly shortening journey to end.

But it did end, and we both got off. We walked away from the bus stop in opposite directions. Then I spent the day listening to lectures from a dietician, and making a variety of fillings for vol-au-vents. Then making the pastry cases themselves. And thinking each time my mind went back to the boy I'd sat next to on the bus – which was pretty much every ten seconds throughout the day – that I'd probably never set eyes on him again. Mostly those negative predictions of ours about the future come true. Only very occasionally are they proved wrong.

He was on the bus next day. I was in the seat beside him almost before my eyes had taken him in. At once, to my enormous surprise, he turned to greet me. 'You were on the bus yesterday,' he said, as though that were a fact I might not have known. I wasn't going to quibble, though. I just saw his eyes as they looked into mine and my heart did something like a somersault.

If eyes really were the windows of the soul, I thought at that moment, then this guy's soul was a thing of beauty indeed. And if that were not the case – then these eyes were worth it for themselves. I still couldn't tell if they were very dark brown or very dark blue. The colour of damsons almost, but unlike any damson I'd seen they shone with inner light. They were smiling. I saw the smile that lit them before my eyes had time to stray to his lips, to receive the confirmation that they were smiling too. I said, 'Hi.' He removed his headphones and smiled a bit more.

'I didn't know you'd seen me yesterday,' I said, unsure of exactly what I meant.

'Oh, I saw you all right,' he said. I wasn't sure exactly what he meant by that either, and maybe neither was he. But after he'd said it his smile became mischievous and twinkly.

'I'm Mick,' I said. It seemed the easiest thing to say next. 'I'm at the catering school.'

'Tom,' he said, and nodded his head very slightly towards me. I felt as absurdly honoured by that gesture as if he'd stood up and made a deep bow. 'Art and design, me.'

'You mean...' It sounded like we were at the same college. 'You're at Butterfield?'

'Yep. Different site from you.'

That explained why we'd walked off in different directions yesterday. Explained why we hadn't met before. Except... 'But the bus. Why haven't I...?'

'New bus,' he said. 'For me, I mean. We've just moved to Wye. Till the weekend I used to travel in from Sturry.'

Diametrically the other side of the town. Of the city. Canterbury. 'You live with your parents?' I don't know why I asked that.

He looked surprised. 'Yeah. Don't you?'

'Course.' I shook my head in the way people do when they've received the answer to a daft question.

'No,' he said, reading my reaction nicely, 'it wasn't a bad question. I mean, I'm nineteen. I could be on my own if I wanted. Or living with someone.' He gave me a smile that hurt.

Live with me, I thought.

'How old are you?' he asked.

'Nineteen.' We eye-balled each other. Both dying to know when the other's birthday fell. Which of us was the older boy. By how much. But neither of us was ready to go there first.

Our bus was slowing for its first stop in the village of Chartham, the driver's braking action setting up a sort of bounding motion. Involuntarily I looked down. No need to tell you why or where.

Yes, I was. So was he. He'd looked down too, I realised at once. I knew this because he gave a little half-embarrassed, half-delighted, snicker of a laugh. How did I manage to read so much into a momentary exhalation of breath, inexperienced as I was? I don't know. Yet I did.

We looked back into each other's face. We were both blushing lightly. I could see the flush on his face, feel it on my own. One of us would have to speak now. Turned out, after a little hiatus, it was me. 'Time of the morning, I guess.'

'I noticed yesterday,' he said shyly.

'I saw yours too,' I said, emboldened just a little by his admission. But not too much. 'I mean just by chance.'

'Yeah,' he said, cautious and prim now. 'Just by chance. Me too.'

A silence fell, during which our eyes dropped again towards each other's lap and our own. Neither of us could think of anything to say. My thoughts were a tangle of writhing snakes. No words I might come up with could conceivably marshal them into any kind of order. It was not an unreasonable guess that the same thing went for him too. Ahead of us the three pinnacled towers of the cathedral now rose above the roofscape, near at hand. I heard and felt, rather than saw, that Tom had put his headphones back on.

If I'd spent the previous day thinking roughly every ten seconds about the lad who'd turned out to be called Tom, then this day, the one of our second encounter, I couldn't get him out of my thoughts at all. My mind went leaping ahead. I imagined us discussing our uncertainties about our sexuality together. I imagined us experimenting a little (at this point I found myself getting hard while stirring a risotto), next I was imagining us on holiday together, just the two of us in some sun-spot abroad – though where the money would come from for such a jaunt I couldn't imagine. Then, by the afternoon I was imagining us setting up in business together, buying a hotel, Tom in charge of the décor and front of house, me taking care of the Michelin-starred cuisine. Then I went home on the bus alone.

I had one thing only to cling onto, but I clung onto it hard. Tom and I had got off the bus together. I went first, as I'd had had the aisle seat, he followed – No, Mick, don't turn round – and we'd parted on the pavement. But we had turned to look at each other for a second. Tom had taken his headphones off again. For just long enough to say to me, 'See you tomorrow, then,' and for me, suddenly too overwhelmed to say anything else, to reply, 'Yeah, sure.'

I clung onto that conversation, picked it over and pulled at it as I lay in bed that night, trying to tease every drop of meaning from it that I could. (Yes, OK, I was clinging onto and pulling at something else at the time: that hardly needs spelling out.) But what did it mean when Tom, or anyone else for that matter, said, 'See you tomorrow.' Was it *I shall see you tomorrow*, a mere statement of fact? *I will see you tomorrow*, statement of intent? Or *I expect, hope, want, wish, yearn, long to see you tomorrow* – a whole spray of exciting ideas to coax forth, in a crescendo of intensity, from that innocent little phrase of just three words.

In the morning I was none the wiser. But when I walked down the bus's narrow gangway I saw him in his accustomed seat, and my empty space beside him and, for the moment at least, that was quite enough.

I slid in alongside. Today I boldly made sure that my hip-bone made contact with his, and firmly enough for him to register the fact. He could make of it what he wanted.

He didn't turn towards me in greeting. Nor did he take his headphones off. I willed myself not to feel disappointed. I willed myself not to turn towards or speak to him. I would sit this out and wait.

I didn't wait long. Nor was I disappointed in the end. At the end of about two seconds actually – though I admit it did feel a bit longer than that – he moved his right thigh infinitesimally, but it was enough for it to engage with my left one along the whole of its jeans-clad length. Then he did turn towards me, removed the headphones. His eyes smiled – more radiant than yesterday – and he said, 'Hi Mick.'

'Oh Tom!' I said. Oh shit, I thought. I'd meant to say Hi Tom, but what had actually come out, compounded by my tone of voice, made it sound like he'd given me not a routine morning greeting but a wonderful surprise present. Although of course that was exactly what he'd done.

He didn't take it back, either. His thigh remained pressed hard against mine as we exchanged a few banal sentences about the weather (which was lovely again this June morning) and the last night's TV. It was only seconds of course before the hardness of our thighs was reinforced by another one – another two to be precise. 'Oh God,' Tom said, with a giggle. There was no pretence on either side now that we didn't know what he meant.

I heard myself say, 'We're going to have to do something about that,' and was shocked by my own boldness. I'd never before today imagined myself saying something like that to a near stranger on a bus. Masturbatory fantasies of sharing sex and a Michelin-starred restaurant with him in the safety of my own bed were one thing, but this...

'How do you mean, do something about it?' he asked. His voice was suddenly unsure of itself. For the first time I heard in it not the cool dude he'd so far presented to me, but a little boy cast suddenly into the sea of adult life, and adrift. I heard him sounding like myself. 'You mean now?' he asked.

I didn't know what I'd meant. I said, 'Yes.'

'We can't very well get them out,' he said, suddenly cool and practical again, though his voice was of necessity a whisper now. The seats in front and behind were all occupied, so were the pair across the aisle.

'We could go for our own, I suppose,' I suggested. Again I was aghast at my daring crudeness. It was my raging boner talking, of course.

'I got a hole in my right pocket,' he said, in a neutral, practical, tone. I had a hole in my left pocket. I told him so. Those two circumstances constituted the most amazing stroke of luck. It could have so easily been the other way around.

I had to roll towards him a bit, so the people across the aisle couldn't see. And it was a bit of a contortionist's act, crossing arms and inserting hands in each other's jeans side-pocket. Especially sitting down. Jeans weren't designed for this. But we got there, just as the bus began to bounce mightily as the driver braked for the Chartham stop. Incredibly I found myself grasping his hot – and by now wet – penis in the dark confines of his underwear, and felt the exquisite delight of his fingers clasping my cock too.

It hardly needs saying that what happened now took only seconds to achieve. It happened to both of us at almost the same instant. I had to prevent myself crying out at the intensity of it, at the hotness of those two sudden floods. I could see that it was just as difficult for him.

Then he kept his hand where it was, and so I kept mine wrapped around his still hard dick for a little time too. That was lovely. We took on passengers at Chartham and they made their way up the aisle towards us. At that point we had to withdraw our hands for reasons which were pragmatic, but in that lingering contact of maybe just thirty seconds the message had been sent, from both sides. We liked that, the message said. We don't regret what we just did.

'What time do you go home in the afternoon?' Tom asked unexpectedly. We'd never met on the bus going back. I'd assumed we went home at different times.

I told him what time I planned to leave. 'My dad's picking me up at the West Gate around then,' he said. 'You can come with us if you want.'

Of course I wanted, even if I was faintly alarmed by the idea of his dad. I said I'd be there. Dad or no dad, it was what I wanted most. I didn't want anything more out of life just then, to be quite frank. Inside my jeans I could feel that everything was soaking wet. Wetter than

I'd been down there since peeing myself as a child. It was going be an uncomfortable walk to college. But I knew the condition was shared by Tom. The discomfort would be his too. And so I didn't care. Instead, as I walked along the pavement, I found in the chafing of my most intimate parts against my thighs a curious and intense kind of joy.

TWO

Life at home, in the small village of Chilham, was quiet. It always had been. Now that I could drive I did at least borrow my parents' car occasionally and go out in the evenings. But I couldn't do this often, and I had no car of my own. There wasn't a lot of money around. At weekends I'd take the bus back into Canterbury sometimes, meet friends and go to a pub, or have a Chinese, perhaps go on to a club after. But my friends weren't especially close ones, and I didn't have a girlfriend. Never had had. I'd never been too sure how you went about getting one of those. Other boys seemed to manage it routinely. But to me it had never happened. Most of my evenings were spent at home, in fact. Watching TV, or playing computer games on my own.

I wasn't an only child. I had two sisters. They were both older than me by some years, though, and had both left home. My father worked on the railway, my mother was a district nurse. Home wasn't really a place where other people – I mean by that my friends – came. But now it seemed I was to be driven back there by Tom's father, the unknown father of someone I also barely knew. Barely knew from the waist up anyway. Would his dad drive me to the door? I wondered. Drop me in the centre of the village on his way to... I didn't know where Tom lived yet exactly, we hadn't got as far as that; he'd just told me that he got on the bus two stops before mine – which in the countryside meant quite some way.

Maybe, if I was going to be delivered to my door I should ask Tom to come in, I thought, as I practised using a blow-torch to glaze crème brûlées darkly. Of course I'd like that. Maybe so would he. It wasn't unreasonable to think that was why he'd made the offer of transport. But then do what? His house might be a palace compared to mine. He'd take one look around perhaps – at the modest living-room, my small bedroom like a furnished box, say something non-committal and take his leave. Never to sit next to me on the bus again.

There was no point thinking like this, I told myself as the afternoon slowly passed. No point crossing bridges before I came to them. All the same, my heart was thumping as I approached the two flint towers of the West Gate. Tom hadn't told me what his dad's car looked like, I realised with alarm. But then there was Tom, jumping half out of something quite large and grey (I'm not good on cars), waving and calling my name.

'So you're one of our new neighbours,' said the back of Tom's father's greying head. I had, of course, taken a seat in the back of the car 'Where exactly are you in the village, Mick?'

'Becket Street,' I mumbled, as if out of the back of my own head. It was not a street in which the village's wealthy lived.

'You'll show us the way when we get near, no doubt,' the head in front of me said blithely. Tom's father, Tom too, had only lived in the neighbourhood a few days. They wouldn't realise the significance of my address. Until they arrived, of course.

'We're just outside the village,' the back of the head said. 'Tom's told you, I'm sure. Bligh House, on the Wye Down road.'

'Dad!' said Tom in a voice of protest. I understood his awkwardness. It was for the same, yet opposite reason as mine. I knew, or knew of, Bligh House, on the Wye Down road. Everybody knew of it. It was huge.

We'd gone through Chartham almost before I'd realised. Chilham was upon us almost as soon. Then there I was, directing Tom's father through and then beyond the picturesque, medieval village square towards the cramped Edwardian terraces of Becket Street. Here goes, I thought. 'Just here,' I said. 'On the left. You can pull in here.'

Then Tom said it, turning round from the front passenger seat to address me between the head-rests. 'Can I come in and see your place?' he asked. He sounded like an eager child of eight, making a new best friend.

'Yeah,' I said. 'Cool. Course you can.' Now I felt like a child of eight. For an awful split second I thought I might cry.

'How will you get back?' the father asked the son. 'Do you want me to...?'

'No problem,' I announced staunchly. This was my moment. I made the most of it. 'I'll run him home in the car.'

My mother was in the living-room with a woman neighbour. It wasn't all that usual a circumstance, so I was particularly glad of it. She wouldn't be able to fuss around Tom and me. 'Tom, a mate of mine,' I introduced him baldly from the hall. 'I'm taking him up to my room.' There. The bridges had been crossed now by both of us. We had nothing to do now but watch them burn behind us.

Tom sat on the one and only chair, the one by the desk I used for studying, and where my computer stuff was. Though he turned it away from the desk, and sat with his legs splayed rather, facing me as I straddled the bottom corner of the bed, from which vantage point I found myself looking slightly up at him.

How strange a thing an angle is. Someone we usually confront face to face, a cashier at the bank perhaps, gives us a new idea about them if we catch them by chance, in profile, at the wheel of a car. So it was with Tom. I'd only seen him full face for a second or two at a time before now, but now I was being treated to this new view of him for a longer time. I liked what I was seeing of course. It became my ambition at that moment to see him from every angle possible. To stare and stare at the different sides of him. I knew, with a deep certainty that I experienced only rarely, that I would like them all.

Wonder of wonders, I understood also at that moment that Tom was thinking and feeling exactly the same.

Tom's gaze wandered over my shoulder for a moment. 'I like the bear,' he said.

I was mortified. Bugsy was a left-over from my childhood. I'd never had the heart to throw him away. Or to kick him out of bed. I still slept with him. I'd never slept with anybody else.

Tom saw my face go red. Read my humiliation there. 'It's OK,' he said. He didn't laugh. He said very seriously, quietly, 'I've got a bear too. Called Simon. He sleeps with me too.'

'When's your birthday?' I asked a few minutes later. We'd talked in the meantime of safer, less freighted things than childhood toys.

'Why?' He laughed. 'Are you going to buy me a present?'

'No. I just want to know.'

'December the sixteenth, then.'

'And you'll be twenty then?'

'Well spotted,' he said. 'And you?'

'I only just turned nineteen last week.'

'Six months between us,' he said slowly. I heard disappointment in his voice, and saw it in his eyes. I realised that he could see the same in mine. I discovered what I hadn't known till then – that we'd both hoped we were twins.

I made the best of it. He was six months older than me, I was six months younger than him. He was the senior one. I wondered what difference that was going to make to whatever happened from now on.

It began to make a difference right then. A guarded look appeared on Tom's face. 'You know, this morning on the bus...'

'Yes,' I said earnestly. It sounded like I was reassuring him I hadn't forgotten the incident.

'I was wondering if you'd... I mean, if you'd done that kind of thing with boys before.'

'Yes and no,' I said cautiously.

The guarded look was replaced with an unguarded smile, which then spluttered into life as a laugh. 'Yes and no?! Whatever's that meant to mean?!'

I laughed too. 'Tell you in a minute. But first, what about you?'

That made him look uncomfortable. 'I guess, actually...' he paused a second, 'I'd have to say the same as you. OK. Maybe we should park that one for now.'

I said, as though it was a matter of supreme unimportance and his answer couldn't have mattered to me less, 'Do you have a girlfriend?'

'Not right now,' he said.

And whatever was that meant to mean...? But I decided that subject could also be parked for now.

Sometimes it happens that a thing is easier for the younger boy to say. So what was said next was said by me. 'Do you want to kiss me?'

I had the impression of a felled tree toppling towards me. I hadn't expected my first kiss to be quite like this. But nobody's first times exactly resemble anyone else's, and this, after all, was mine.

It was as though he had a flying squirrel's brake-flaps between spread arms and legs. Because he managed to slow as he flew down towards me, and landed on me lightly, not with a crunch, as he pushed me back onto the bed. His lips hit mine, their target, first time, square on. I smelt, rather than tasted them. The savour of them would have crushed any resistance I might have felt or made. It was an academic point. No resistance came.

His tongue found its way past the portcullis of my teeth into the warm safety of my mouth. Mine found its way by a similar path into his. How did we know how to do this, never having done it – either of us – before? The same way the birds know how to weave their nests. Like birds' nests our two mouths were cosy and warm.

I felt Tom's hands ransacking the curls my hair made around my ears, and flattening those that covered my crown. My own hands, which seemed to have intentions of their own, meanwhile explored his shoulders, kneaded his neck, caressed his collar-bones.

Then I was aware his hands had abandoned me. Abandoned my head and neck at any rate. Though they soon turned up elsewhere. I felt them mole their ways between our pressed-together bellies, then grapple with my waistband stud and with my zip.

I thought suddenly of my mother, just one floor below, with sudden alarm. Alarm turned to panic a second later. She wasn't one floor below but at the door. Knocking, thank God, not turning the handle and coming in. But this was bad enough. 'Can I get you boys anything?'

Tom sprang up off me and propelled himself backwards into his chair. God knows how he managed the physics and mechanics of that. It was like watching a film on fast rewind. Me, I was sitting upright on the corner of the bed without knowing how I managed that either, and scrabbling to re-fasten my fly. 'We're OK thanks,' I heard myself say breathlessly, while Tom and I held each other's appalled stare. 'I'll be taking Tom back to Bligh House as soon as Dad's back with the car.'

We continued to hold each other's gaze as we listened to Mum's vanquished footsteps descending the stairs, but were still too unnerved and shaken to exchange a smile.

A moment later we heard the return of my dad's car, and felt each other's relief almost physically. 'You want to drive me back to mine?' Tom asked in a diffident voice. 'There'll be a meal.'

Then we were tramping down the stairs. 'I'm taking Tom back home to Bligh House,' I called through the open living-room door. 'If it's OK to have the car. I may be back late. Don't wait tea.'

Bligh House was not at all what I'd expected. It was big, yes, but not in the slightest bit chilly or grand. It was as homely as my own house – just four times the size. In the kitchen two immense tabby cats snoozed on the shelf behind the Aga stove. Two young French teenagers romped boisterously round about. Tom's mother was teaching them English, Tom explained. Taking in foreign students, feeding, housing and teaching them, helped to make ends meet. Meanwhile it was now six o'clock. Would I like a drink? I most certainly would, I said.

We took our beers out into the garden, Tom and I. No-one tried to follow us out. We sat at a garden table, on heavy wooden seats. The garden sloped down the hillside that was called Wye Down. We sat overlooking the broad plain of the river Stour spread out before us, the distant town of Ashford, and the Romney Marsh beyond. In the far distance lay the sea.

'You won't believe this,' Tom said, as we looked down approvingly on the view. 'But we've another place in Scotland just as big as this.' He looked sideways at me. 'I didn't mean to boast. I'm sorry. It's just that I want to impress you somehow. I'm not sure how to, though. Oh shit.' He looked down. 'I'm talking like a complete arse-hole.'

'No, you're not,' I said. I wanted to express my feeling towards him, the fondness I felt at that moment, by reaching out and giving his cock a squeeze, but I was just too far away. To have stood up, taken a pace or two and then done it would have robbed the gesture of its meaning and given it another one – which I felt could be better explored a little later on. Besides, his parents might have appeared at any moment.

But I think he got the message anyway. Somehow. It was getting to be like that between us. He gave me another oddly sideways, crooked smile and said, 'I like your house, you know. I like your room.'

Cheekily I asked him, 'Will I get to see yours?'

'Hell's armies won't stop that happening,' he said. Then his brow furrowed. 'Though I'm not quite sure how.' He thought another moment. 'Can you stay the night with me? There's two beds in my room. No questions will be asked.'

The invitation made my heart soar. Only to flutter back to earth a moment later. 'There's the little matter of my dad's car.'

'Oh bollocks. I see.' He frowned at the distant view a moment. Then his face brightened and he looked at me. 'OK. There's a good half hour before dinner still. Here's the plan...'

It wasn't difficult. I phoned my parents, told them I was staying over. Then we dove in convoy back to Becket Street, Tom in his father's, me in my father's, car. Left Dad's car for him in the morning. Grabbed toothbrush and a change of clothes, then Tom drove me back to his. We arrived there just as asparagus and white wine were being served. These things are easy when you know how.

THREE

Family supper with someone else's family. A family you don't know. I didn't know Tom, come to that. I mean I knew the important thing. That we clicked. Really clicked in some big way that I was yet to fathom. Oh yes, and he had a nice cock, but now I'm being flippant. On the other hand we had hardly begun, in our conversations in my bedroom and in the car, to get hold of the other stuff that in normal circumstances comes at the beginning. Where had he gone to school? Which football team did he support? Did he even like football? Most boys won't admit that they don't when that is the case. It fingers them as gay.

At least there were a lot of us around the table, which prevented the occasion being too intimate or intense. Tom and me, Tom's parents, his kid brother and kid sister, the two French kids, one of each sex, and a woman teacher who was temporarily living in and helping to tutor the foreign kids. That made nine. You can hide more easily in a number like that.

After supper – though I suppose I should say dinner, there were three courses after all – there was the question of what we'd do, Tom and I, before bedtime came. There was no doubt about what we'd do when we went to bed. But, though no eyebrows were going to be raised about us sharing Tom's room, we would certainly have set tongues wagging had we headed off to bed straight after dinner. After all, it was barely half past eight.

'We could go to the pub, I suppose?' Tom said with a query in his voice.

'Which one?'

'The one in Wye's nearer than Chilham,' he said a bit uncertainly. 'I haven't been in any round here yet.'

That was a point. The Tickled Trout in Wye was a place I'd visited rarely. I certainly wasn't known there. In Chilham, of course, I was. To go into either of the pubs there with a stranger would have given rise to curiosity at least. But to go to the Tickled Trout with Tom would be a more neutral experience. We'd be taken for two straight lads who'd just popped in for a drink. Or would we? Would we already be taken for...? No, I didn't want to think the thought. I wasn't sure how we would behave towards each other in a public house, even in one where neither of us would be recognized. Weighing all this up in a second, during which Tom looked at me expectantly, I decided we weren't quite ready for the exposure of a pub. 'Maybe we could just sit out in your garden with a beer and chill?' I suggested a bit diffidently.

Tom's face broke into a smile of relief. 'That's what I hoped you'd say,' he said.

We took our beers out to the place we'd sat earlier, looking out over Kent and Sussex towards the west. Walking through the garden to get there this second time, I noticed the place was full of colour. Crazy I hadn't registered this before. My attention too intensely focused on Tom, I guess. But now here they were: the flowers of June. Dancing columbines, pink, yellow and deep blue. Purple lupins and almost indecently swollen crimson peony heads. We left them behind us as we made for our almost secluded – though not secluded enough – seats among the green. But that brief journey through intense colour remained etched on my retina, together with the message it carried. That summer had come, or was on the brink of coming. For me at least. And, I hoped, for Tom. At least it would come if we got things – got everything – just right.

'Why did you move here?' I asked when we'd sat down and cracked our beers. It seemed a practical way of dealing with the pre-bed gap: catch up on all the humdrum stuff we hadn't done before. And I did want to know.

Tom laughed. 'You'll think this sounds crap. But I'll tell you anyway. Dad came into money. We weren't badly off before. But the house in Sturry wasn't that big. Not for all of us and foreign students too. An uncle of my dad's died last year. No kids of his own. And so...'

'And the place in Scotland?'

'That too. He was a bit of a baronial chief, my great-uncle. Now – weirdly – the place is ours. You must come up some time.'

I said cheers and took a swig of beer, feeling morose for a moment. The difference between *You must come up some time* and *We're going there on Tuesday, please join us, nine o'clock train* is an infinite one as we all know.

He said, 'We'll be going up there, sorting the place out, soon as term's ended and the students have gone home. That's in two weeks' time.' He stopped and looked down at the ground between his spread thighs. 'I don't suppose...?'

'Don't suppose what?' I asked, not daring to guess what he was about to propose. That I'd be able to come in and feed the cats maybe.

'Nah,' he shook his head. 'You'll have things planned.'

I'd nothing planned. I wanted to say this, throwing myself around his neck sobbing, and then wail, please take me with you. I didn't. I said brusquely, 'Nothing special, I don't think. Why?'

He turned towards me and to my astonishment I saw his eyes were glistening. 'It's just that I'd love it – I mean, how wonderful that would be – if you could come too.' And I suddenly saw the effort that it had cost him to say all that. And how brave he'd just been. And how close we both were to breaking down.

'I'd like that too,' I said, sounding cool and practical, and not at all as though my world had just exploded into a kaleidoscope of colour and joy. 'You're on. I'll sort it with Mum and Dad.'

'And I'll sort it with mine.'

'Well, that's all settled, then,' I said, as if we'd just closed a business deal. But then I allowed myself to give him a smile. I think it must have been a rather radiant one. To judge from the one that he beamed at me in return.

We angled ourselves a little more towards each other as we sat on our uncomfortable wooden chairs. By now we were longing to fall into each other's arms – and legs and other things. We couldn't yet. The sound of the younger teenagers playing tag or something around the lawns and through the shrubberies behind us kept reminding us we weren't alone. And from time to time one or other of them would materialise between the bushes that half-shielded us, and say something to us, either in English or in French, depending who they were. Meanwhile the sun remained obstinately high in the evening sky. It was mid-June so it was only to be expected. But we felt unable yet to go to bed. Not while the sun stayed up. Not at age nineteen.

Tom went back to the house to get us a second beer. Alone for a few moments I allowed myself the luxury of a dip into my jeans pocket with my hand. Gave my cock a reassuring feel. It was semi-hard. I wasn't surprised at that. I tried to think ahead to what new experiences the night ahead of me might bring. The difficulty of that thought made me gasp, though not in an unpleasant way. Then I heard the sound of Tom coming back through the bushes, and withdrew my hand from my pocket. He appeared with two fresh cans of beer. 'Something's put a smile on your face,' he said, looking me up and down.

'Yeah,' I said. Then, cheaply, but I couldn't resist it, 'I hope it'll soon be putting a smile on yours.'

We seemed to float back through the garden on our way indoors. Was that the beer? Or the heightened emotional and sexual state we were both in? Or just that June dusk thing, when white flowers throb and pulse at you through the scented gloom, and objects escape from the confinements of size and place as the light fades. Or a mixture of the three.

We made our way upstairs unchallenged. TV was on in another room, but the door was closed. We didn't do a public goodnight. Thank God, it seemed that wasn't expected in this household. We went into Tom's room and closed the door behind us. I'd been in here before dinner, for twenty seconds or so, just to dump my overnight things and have a pee in … Tom's private bathroom. I'd never come across such a thing in a friend's house before. And certainly not in my own humble home.

But now – but now the door was shut behind us and we were alone. Sharing that special aloneness that belongs to lovers at the moment when they are just becoming lovers, and are acknowledging for the first time that that is what they are.

I'd already clocked that the two beds were single ones, and were positioned alongside opposite walls. Two lockers and a window separated them. But that was a detail that could be dealt with in time. I'd also noticed Simon, the teddy bear I'd been told about, tucked up in the left-hand bed. But now Tom and I had eyes for nothing in the room except each other. We stood facing each other about a foot apart – a foot that might have been a mile just then, it seemed – both wondering what would happen next.

'You look good, mate,' I said.

'And you look fucking great.' There was a hiatus. Neither of us moved a muscle. Then he picked up the gauntlet that was his six months' seniority, and said what he had to. 'Come here.'

I slid forward into his arms and, except that we were now vertical not horizontal, we continued from exactly the point at which we'd had to break off when we'd been on my bed and my mum was on the stairs.

With one hand I explored his buttocks, caressing first one and then the other, and running the blade of my hand momentarily along the little valley in between. The pert twin domes felt wonderful. Perfect, in fact. I was in awe of them. I had no idea if my own butt was a good feature in any way. Whether another person would discover in it the sensual beauty that I found in Tom's. But just then the sensation of another's hand groping for the first time in my life my own backside told me that Tom was embarked on a similar voyage of discovery. For better or worse.

To my astonishment I heard him whisper, lips against my neck, 'You're just beautiful.'

My voice so thin a whisper that it was next to silent, I said, 'You too.'

I felt his other hand clutch my cock urgently through my jeans. Was I hard? You bet I was. Was he? Of course. For my own hand had, like lightning, made a grab for his. It was sticking vertically upwards, twelve o'clock, pointing towards, though not quite reaching, the top stud of his jeans. Mine, though equally tumescent, had met with some obstacle among the seams of my underwear and was stopped for now at about half past nine.

We weren't going to let that little difference last for long. I got his jeans undone in a second or two, pulling them and his underpants down to his knee in one yank, and relishing the sight of his dick springing out and up, and the sound of the little thwack it made as it hit his belly. A second later and Tom had released my trapped dick too, and it responded in the same way.

In my eagerness I grabbed Tom's and started urgently to pull the skin back and forth. He stopped me with a hand and with a giggle. 'No, wait,' he said. 'Let's get undressed properly. Get horizontal. Then take it from there. If we let it all go at once...'

'It might be twenty minutes before we were ready to go again,' I said, and for the first time in my life heard myself sounding ever so slightly camp.

But we got undressed anyway. Actually we undressed each other. More clumsy. Slower. But more fun. And there wasn't that much to do. We had no ties or shirts on. Just T-shirts to pull up over each other's head and throw onto a chair.

Next... Well, there was nothing else for it. We had to unlace each other's trainers. Unlacing another guy's shoes, and removing first them and then his socks, may not be an infallible indicator of love, but it's a hell of a sign of commitment to what you intend to do together next.

After that the last part was easy. Pull off each other's half-mast jeans and half-shed underwear and throw those too on the chair. Then we took half a pace back, to stand a moment and admire what we had done. Our handiwork. Each other, in short.

Tom was not very tall. I don't think I've mentioned this. About five foot seven. Which I am too. A source of solidarity, that. Not very muscular, actually, either of us, but neither were we so skinny as to have bony elbows and knees. But we were only nineteen, and so we each still displayed a rib or two. We'd probably have balanced a set of scales. There the resemblances ended. His hair was raven black, mine mouse. I had almost none on my body, except under my arms of course, and my little circlet of pubes. Tom's bush, by contrast, was a great triangle of black thatch, up from which a wavy plume arose, climbing past his navel, to divide into two symmetrical fans of chest hair. It made him look very advanced for nineteen. Left me looking child-like by comparison. Of course, he did have that significant six months' start on me.

We admire in others the things we lack in ourselves. So I was envious of Tom's hirsute upper body. We forget that this works both ways. 'Oh wow,' Tom said, and I realised that my boy-like hairlessness was as big a turn on for him.

As for our cocks, which our eyes had strayed to immediately, before taking in the big picture, and to which our gaze now returned, they were reassuringly alike. Respectably sized rather than enormous, elegant rather than startling. Both of us had been allowed to retain the foreskins we'd been born with; we both sported a small but perfectly formed pair of balls that nestled in fur.

It had needed barely a second to take all this in. But even that had been too long a time without touching. We moved in towards each other a second time. What a difference a layer of clothes makes! Never before had I felt a warm bare chest – with or without hair – pressed up against mine. Nor thighs nor, more comically, amusingly, naked knees. To say nothing of that thing in the heart of our embrace, that double-barrelled shot-gun thing, six inches in length, so warm, so hard yet soft – strong yet delicate at the same time. And about which the most amazing thing of all was this: that as our two dicks stood clamped together between our tummies I couldn't tell – at least the sensitive skin of my tummy couldn't – which was mine and which was his.

'Come to bed,' he said.

He pulled back the duvet from the bed that Simon wasn't sleeping in (I'm still not sure of the psychology behind that) and we jumped in between the sheets. Jumped literally, me first, then him. He pulled up the duvet till it covered us. Then (as the younger of us two, I thought it fell to me to be the first to admit this) I said, 'I've never gone to bed with anyone else before.'

Now he could tell me, if he wanted to, that he'd slept with any number of people, of either sex or both, or... 'I haven't either,' he said quietly, for a moment turning his head away. He sounded even more ashamed of the fact than I had done.

'And now here we are,' I said. I grabbed hold of him around the shoulders and cuddled and shook him like I was playing with a dog, and he did the same to me.

'I don't know if I'm gay,' he said suddenly, sounding almost frightened of the thought.

'Does it matter if you are or not?' I said. A bit urgently too. I didn't want us to go off the boil right now. 'Does it matter whether I am? Because, honestly, I don't know that about myself. I haven't had enough chances to find out one way or the other. Let's just do this anyway. Even if just the once. I don't want to stop now.'

I didn't think I could stop now, actually. I was only a minute away, I think, from spontaneously coming all over his sheets.

'Do this?' he said. 'Do what? I'm not sure I...'

'Just do what we did this morning on the bus,' I said. This morning! It seemed a lifetime ago. 'Only holding each other this time. And staying...' I wanted to say something like, *staying holding onto each other afterwards,* and then perhaps wanting to add, *for ever and ever,* but fortunately I wasn't able to get those words, or any others, out.

And so we began gently to stroke each other's cock. Concentrating on this, awed by the novelty of the experience, mercifully took away the urgency I'd felt a moment before. No longer was I in danger of shooting all over the shop all at once. We took our time, enjoying each other's crescendo of sensation through the nuzzling movements of legs, arms and head, the quivering of the other's tummy, hearing each other's progress towards the summit in the whimpery, breathy sounds that were all that was left of voice.

Then, when we did come, almost simultaneously again, lying on our sides, belly to belly in tight embrace, it was as if a dam had burst inside me. A bigger dam than the physical ones – the pair of them – that had hot-showered our chests and bellies and flooded the bottom sheet. I knew, as we continued our embrace for a long time in the form of a kiss, not caring whether we mopped up or not, or when, that everything my heart was feeling, Tom's was too.

In the morning we entered the kitchen together for early breakfast. We had to make the bus for college after all. Tom's mum greeted us brightly. 'I hope you both slept well.'

I didn't dare attempt to catch Tom's eye. 'Well, I certainly did,' I said.

Anthony McDonald

FOUR

How odd it was, the bus ride into Canterbury that morning, how different. We sat in our usual places, Tom and I, pressed up alongside each other rather firmly, because that is how we felt we wanted to be. Actually we wanted to be in each other's arms but that simply wasn't possible here and now. Same bus, same route, same Tom and me... Except we weren't the same Tom and me. We were utterly changed from the people we had been yesterday. Like birds in a nest box after the box has been shaken and turned upside down. We were disoriented by what had happened to us. We didn't even know what had happened. Well, we knew we'd slept together. But that was all.

I remember that neither of us got a hard-on during that short journey to college. We'd woken at first light for a repeat of what we'd done before going to sleep. Then, after dozily caressing each other for a couple of hours there had been another encore before we got up. We didn't actually need to do it again on the bus this morning. That was one difference from yesterday.

The other changes were bigger ones. They came in the form of a series of questions that I was turning over and over in my head as we bounced through the sunlit Kent downs. I had no doubt at all that Tom was grappling with the same thorny things. What we had done: did it make us gay? Was that the label we'd have to wear from now on? What had become of Tom and me: were we lovers now? Boyfriends? Or just two boys who'd got caught up in a moment's madness? Just good friends?

I thought the last of those was the least probable scenario. It was slightly more probable, I thought glumly, that we'd quickly drop each other, travel to college at different ends of the bus and never speak again. But as I stared that eventuality in the face I knew that I couldn't bear that to happen. That I'd work hard to make sure it did not. My encounter with Tom had been the most precious things I'd had up till now. A first flash of gold in my pan of silt. I wasn't easily going to throw it away.

But that brought me to the most immediate question. What happened now? Where did Tom and I go from here?

What happened now was that we reached the bus station in Canterbury, and everybody who remained on board, including Tom and me, stood up to get off. Tom would walk one way, I the other. Today was Friday. Ahead of us lay the weekend...

We hadn't spoken for several minutes. I'd been deeply inside myself, contemplating those difficult questions, and so – I had no doubt – had Tom. On the pavement we turned and faced each other. Tom looked too anxious to manage a smile. 'What are you doing this evening?' he asked quickly, nervously, fearful of what I might say.

I'd arranged to meet some mates in one of the city centre pubs. I'd almost forgotten that. Almost forgotten I had other mates. Anyway, it would be easy to text my excuses. 'Nothing,' I said. Then, laying my cards bravely on the table – it was one of the bravest moments of my life actually – I said, 'I'd really like to see you.'

The relief on his face was overwhelming. Though the moment was too serious, too important, for his relief to take the form of a smile. 'I'd really like that too,' he said gravely. 'We could meet at the Tickled Trout, maybe. 'Since nobody knows us there.' He thought for a moment. 'Will you be able to get your dad's car?'

Even if I had to steal it from under his nose. Even if I had to fight him for it. 'No probs,' I said.

'Look, gotta go,' he said. 'And you too. See you in the Trout at nine?'

'You bet,' I said.'

We met sooner than that. When I returned to the bus station that afternoon, there was Tom. It shouldn't have surprised me, but it did. Simply because our return journeys hadn't coincided earlier in the week. But there was no reason why they shouldn't do from time to time, even if we didn't plan things that way.

So we travelled back together, the way we'd come that morning. By now we found ourselves talking easily again. We exchanged numbers and email – something we hadn't though to do up till now. We slightly modified our evening plan. Tom would come and pick me up from Becket Street, and we'd drive together to the Tickled Trout. If by the end of the evening we'd drunk more than was safe for the longer drive back to my place – well, Bligh House was pretty near the Tickled Trout, and there were still two beds in Tom's room... It sounded a brilliant plan.

My parents weren't fazed by the arrival of Tom, a young man they'd little more than glimpsed the day before, to whisk their only son away in a smart car as soon as the evening meal was done. At least, they weren't fazed this first time.

Tom drove rather fast towards Wye. Wanting to impress me, of course. He really didn't need to try and impress me; he'd already impressed me in a pretty major way. But all the same I was touched. That he wanted to impress me... Well, it brought on a feeling I didn't quite recognize, as I don't think I'd felt it before. It was an indescribably wonderful feeling, but it somehow hurt. I didn't have a name for it as yet...

Coming round the bend into the village we overtook a long line of parked cars. At least that's what we thought we were doing. At one point, on the next bend, a van was parked, halfway onto the pavement, on the other side of the road. 'Bloody hell, what parking!' Tom complained as we squeaked through the gap with a bare inch to spare. But a second later, rounding that blind bend completely, we realised our mistake. We'd just overtaken, not a line of parked cars, but the queue for the level crossing, and we were now ourselves stopped by the closed barrier, but on the wrong side of the road, and eye-balling the driver of the front car in the queue the other side. 'Oh,' Tom said. I had nothing to add.

As soon as the barrier began to lift, Tom put his foot down fast and we revved off, twisting into the gap between the car in front and the one we were alongside, just as that gap itself began to close. We got through without losing any paintwork. Just. But we didn't escape a barrage of hoots – and shouts from the wound-down windows of pretty well every other car in sight. A few seconds later we were turning into the car-park of the Tickled Trout, and so, embarrassingly, was the car immediately behind.

That car parked on the opposite side of the car-park to the one we chose, for which we were thankful, but its occupants' path to the pub's front door then converged with ours. 'What did you think you were fucking doing?' one of them, presumably the driver, called as soon as we were close enough.

'I made a mistake,' said Tom. 'It does happen. Anyway, apologies.' We hung back and let him and his party precede us through the door. They were four pretty fit lads in their mid-twenties. A bit rough looking. They didn't say anything further to us, or turn back to look at us. Though we heard the one who'd spoken say to his companions, 'Fucking little poofs,' as they went through the door. We decided not to reply.

The interior of the pub was bright. Exposed oak beams in walls and ceiling were golden rather than black. The room was spacious, and the bar was long. So we didn't have to stand cheek by cheek or shoulder to shoulder with the men from the other car as we queued for our drinks, but were able to ignore them, as they ignored us, standing at different ends of the long counter. When we'd got our pints of Spitfire we walked out with them, through a large conservatory, onto the riverside lawn. And there, on the grassy slope, we sat watching the river as dusk began to fall. On the grass, our arms hugging our pulled-up knees.

Swallows skimmed the current that flowed fast through tresses of weed. A swan paddled with cygnets between two grass-plumed islets. And in the shallow, crystal clear chalk stream, speckly brown, almost translucent trout hung, all heads pointing into the current, maintaining their stationary positions with gentle swimming movements of fins and graceful twitches of their tails. Beside us rose the small Gothic arches of a stone bridge that went back to medieval times.

'It's beautiful here,' I said. You're beautiful here was what I meant.

'Kind of perfect,' Tom replied, still staring out at the stream. I could hardly bear to look at him at that moment. The sight of him made me quiver inside; this was all so wonderful that it hurt.

Then Tom said, 'Why do people have to spoil things?'

'Who? How do you mean?'

'That c**t from the car.'

I'd almost forgotten. 'Don't think about it,' I said. 'It's nothing.' I gestured towards what was happening to the river just a few feet away 'Water under the bridge.'

'He called us fucking poofs,' Tom said.

'And you just called him a c**t,' I said. 'So what? Someone we don't know and will never want to care about thinks we're a pair of fairies. You think maybe he's right. Is that the long and the short of it?'

Tom looked at me unhappily. 'Dunno. What do *you* think?'

'I don't know, Tom,' I said. 'I really don't. I haven't enough experience to go on. Of any kind. Anyway, does it matter? What people call us, I mean. Who needs labels around their necks? Placed there by themselves or other people. Can't we just do whatever we want to do together as just you and me? Can't it be just a Tom and Mick thing, a Mick and Tom thing? Fuck what anybody else says or thinks.' That was quite a long, quite a vehement speech for me. I'd surprised myself. And I saw I'd surprised Tom too. To my relief, in quite a good way.

He smiled at me. 'You're great, you are. You do me so much good. Of course you're right. You know...' He wrinkled his nose. I hadn't seen him do this before. It looked cute. 'Right now I'm wishing the only two people on the planet were me and you.'

I certainly wished we could be the only two people on the riverside lawn. I ached to fall across him and then the two of us roll together, unbuttoning each other frenziedly on the grass. But we were not alone. There were heterosexual couples, parents with young kids...

'We'll find places,' I said. 'Places we can be alone together. Just the pair of us.' I felt a thrill as I heard myself say that last phrase. It sounded like a commitment to something. To him. It was like standing in a crowded church, I thought suddenly, and saying, 'I do.'

He said, in a tone of the greatest wonder, 'And I've only known you five days.' He was saying it to himself rather than to me.

I tried to think back to four days ago, to five days ago. To what life had been like before I met him. I could hardly remember such a time at all.

He said, 'Have you ever fucked anyone, Mick?'

'No,' I said. We'd already admitted to each other that we'd never slept with anyone else before. But of course you don't have to sleep with someone in order to fuck them. He was just making double sure. 'No, not even up against a wall. What about you?'

'Ditto,' Tom said. 'And nobody's fucked me either, before you ask me that too. You?'

'Same goes for me,' I said.

'Pathetic, aren't we,' he said. 'Two little virgins of nineteen.'

'I don't see that makes us pathetic,' I protested. 'Just because we haven't had pene... penetrative sex with anyone.' (I'd never said that word out loud before.) 'I liked what we did last night, actually. Don't know about you but it had a pretty powerful impact on me.' I knew enough about him already to know he wouldn't disagree.

'Yeah,' he said. 'Powerful doesn't say the half of it. It was...'

We made love. That's what he wanted to say but didn't dare. It's what I wanted him to say. I wanted to say it myself. What cowards we were.

'I know,' I said. 'And I want to do that again and again with you. Don't care, really, if we ever do any other kind of thing or not. It's what suits us – the pair of us – that counts.' I'd slipped in that phrase *the pair of us* again. 'In fact,' I said, after taking a seriously big swallow of beer, 'if we have a couple more of these, our parents'll take a dim view of you driving me all the way home. Then I'll have to stay over at yours. End of story.'

Tom downed the last third of his pint in one long swallow. 'You better get the next one in, then,' he said, the wicked twinkle rekindling in his eyes.

It was the accident of hearing those two words together – fucking poofs – that had got to him, I realised. Correction. They'd got to me too. Because, what did poofs do? They fucked other poofs. People who fucked poofs were poofs themselves. QED. Whereas, if you didn't actually fuck another man, if another man didn't fuck you, perhaps you weren't a poof at all. So that was OK then.

Except it wasn't. An incredible thing had happened for Tom and me. No penetration of any kind had taken place, yet we were somehow bonded anyway. We were just hung up on a name, anxious about how to identify ourselves now. We didn't know how to say exactly who and what we were, or explain to ourselves what it was we'd done. We just knew that we liked the way things were going. Whatever might happen to derail things in the future, we loved the way that things were now. This time four nights ago we'd never met. We'd never heard each other's name. It was an incredible thought.

'So tell me,' Tom said, in a half-teasing voice that was also shy. 'What you didn't tell me yesterday.' Though it was dark now we were still out on the floodlit river bank, lying stretched out now, though propped on elbows and twisted round so we were looking in each other's eyes. Our pint glasses (we were on round three by now) stood precariously on the grass by our sides.

'What didn't I tell you yesterday?' I asked, also half teasing. I was pretty sure I knew.

'You know,' he said.

'What? The same as what you didn't tell me?'

'Probably,' he said.

'You mean when I answered yes and no to a question of yours, and you did too.'

'That's the one,' Tom said, slowly nodding his head. 'God, you're slow sometimes.'

'And so are you.' I balled up a handful of plucked grass and flung it towards him. It fell apart and got nowhere near him of course.

'You want to tell me now?'

'May as well,' I said. I hadn't drunk the best part of three pints when I'd stonewalled his question yesterday. I hadn't known him then as well as I did now.

FIVE

'It was something that happened on holiday last year,' I said. 'Not that much happened. I mean, really nothing happened...'

'Just get on with it,' said Tom.

'We were in Majorca.' I looked at Tom's face. 'I know you'll think that's down market, but...'

'I don't. You get me wrong. Anyway, most of Majorca's beautiful. I've been there too. Tell the story.'

'Me and my parents were in this hotel. Anyway they'd gone to bed one evening and I was still sitting around the pool, finishing a beer. There was a guy at the hotel, with another guy a few years older than him. And he, the younger one, was a couple of years older than me. I did sometimes wonder if they were a gay couple. But they didn't do anything obvious to show they were. Not in public anyway. And lots of men go on holiday with a friend. Doesn't mean they're gay.

'We'd chatted sometimes, the three of us. They both seemed to like me. The younger one, especially. And to be honest, I thought he looked nice. He was tall, blond, with a tennis player's physique...

'Anyway, that evening he came out of the bar and onto the poolside just as I was thinking about going back inside and up to bed. He saw me and came over. Asked, could he join me. Of course I said yes. There was an atmosphere between us. I noticed at once. It was ... well, OK, it was sexy. Can't explain how. Just that he knew that and I knew that. We talked about nothing really for a minute or two, then he saw my beer was empty and said, "Come for a walk? Just to the bottom of the grounds and back."'

I saw Tom's grin grow wide.

'OK,' I said. 'Yes, I sort of knew, and sort of didn't. You know how it is.' He had the grace to stop grinning and to nod.

'Anyway, we walked together down past the tennis courts and through a garden where there were games like giant chess and mini-golf among the trees. Which were all full of fairy lights at night, by the way. Then finally we got to the end of the garden, and found ourselves standing between shadows the palm trees cast and also partly in patches of... OK, you're not to laugh. There was a full moon...' Tom did a sort of war-whoop of laughter. 'So,' I carried on regardless, 'there were patches of silver moonlight all around. That's just how it was.'

'OK,' said Tom. I could see his struggle with the muscles of his face.

'Then he turned to me – his name was George, by the way, and he said, "Isn't this beautiful?" He added, "And you're beautiful." He took me in his arms. I didn't resist. No man had ever done that to me before. The next thing I knew, we were kissing. On the lips. But with mouths closed. Honestly – when you kissed me properly yesterday, that was the first time for me...'

'Just get on with the story,' Tom said with a little smile. And I noticed him absently caress his dick at that moment with the hand that wasn't propping him up. It was just for a second, but I did notice.

'Then I could feel him pushing his groin into mine, and realised I was doing the same to him. I could feel our two cocks through our clothes and realised we were both hard. And the next thing that happened – well, it came from me. I'd had my two arms around him. Now I took one away and moved it to his fly. I poked a finger in between the studs of his fly and felt his prick there. Touched the skin of it. He had no underwear on so I got there at once. It came as a shock. You can imagine. But it was nice, of course. Then – I can't imagine what made me so bold...'

'I can,' said Tom, poker-faced, my senior by six big months.

'Well anyway, I undid his fly and took out his cock. It was massive. Put mine in the shade.'

'Mine too, in that case,' said Tom, sounding a bit less pleased.

'I'm just telling you how it was,' I said. 'You keep saying, go on with the story, and that's just how it was. So don't complain.' He took that as the joke it was meant to be, I'm pleased to say. 'And then he took mine out. Nobody'd ever held it before. I can tell you – it did feel great. I thought for a moment I was going to come in his hand, there and then. But then almost at once he took his hand away. "I shouldn't be doing this," he said. "My boyfriend back at the hotel..."

'I let go of his cock too then. I don't know if I did that reluctantly, or if I was glad of the chance to get out of a situation I really wasn't sure I wanted to be in. I said, "Then I shouldn't be doing this either." Then we slowly unwound our other arms from each other's waist – stuffed our cocks away, which wasn't easy – and walked back through the garden to the hotel.'

'And that was that?' Tom wanted to know.

'We smiled at each other during the next few days when we passed in the hotel grounds or in the town. Said hallo and things. Nothing else happened.'

'Come on,' said Tom. He downed the last of his pint and began to get up from the ground.

'Hey,' I said. 'You haven't told me your story yet.'

'It can wait for another time. Yours was a sweet and rather lovely one. Mine's not. This isn't the moment for it. I've got better ideas in mind.' He was now standing and as I started to stand too, he pulled me up the rest of the way towards him and, heedless of the last straggler customers also out on the lawn, gave me a quick kiss as he rumpled my hair. 'Let's go home now.'

'Bligh House?'

'Of course,' he said, and I was thrilled he'd used the word home to describe the place where we were going to stay the night together. His home was my home now. Wherever Tom was, I thought, a bit fuddled by the beer, would be my home for ever.

Tom's driving was a bit erratic on the way back, and it wasn't helped by his constant attempts to grab my cock and stroke my thigh through the fabric of my jeans, nor by my doing the same things to him. But it was little more than a mile back to Bligh House, and we made it safely. We spilled out of the car, went back to it, remembering we hadn't locked it, then tumbled in through the front door. Tom's father was crossing the hall. 'You again?' he said, addressing me. Then he smiled warmly. 'Nice to see you, Mick. You're welcome here as often as you like. And I hear you may be joining us on our Scottish jaunt in a couple of weeks. We'll look forward to that.' And with that he disappeared into the kitchen, removing with him any possible threat I might have thought he represented to my friendship with his son. For the moment at any rate.

Now we stood together in Tom's bedroom again. Would we repeat the ceremony we'd performed last night: the ritual removal of each other's clothes? Or would we go for the more practical option of undressing ourselves? There was a little delay as we both looked at each other, both asking ourselves that same question. Then Tom said, 'May I unlace your shoes?' in the gentlest voice I'd heard him use, even to me. Without waiting for an answer he knelt at my feet and did just that, removing them, plus my socks, one by one, as I lifted them in turn off the floor. Then I knelt at his feet and did the same to him. I pulled one trick that hadn't occurred to him. I nuzzled his crotch with the top of my head, and felt his stiffness through his jeans against my hair.

And so we repeated the ritual of the previous night. There wasn't much to deal with once the socks had gone. Just T-shirt, jeans and underpants. But we spun it out a bit, so we could admire each other's modest physique piece by piece along the way. In a way, of course, in doing this we were admiring ourselves. If Tom's unthreatening little muscles and modest stature made his nude form beautiful in the eyes of another man then the same clearly went for me. Whether, in my skinned-rabbit naked state I would have appeared attractive to a woman – something about which I'd wondered anxiously until just two days ago – I no longer remotely cared.

It was a hot night. We dispensed with the services of the duvet, and lay naked on the bottom sheet. We kept the curtains open. In the middle of the countryside, halfway up the hillside, the house was overlooked by no-one except the birds. There was a moon, and it lit the contours of our bodies as we lay there, caressing each other lightly; it turned us into silver-ridged, black-shadowed landscapes, or into statues of marble, that nevertheless lived, moved and breathed. For some time we left our erections teasingly, tantalisingly unexplored, enjoying the delay. They seemed ready to remain in their inflated state for ever if necessary, while the moon caught the silver threads that slowly spun out of them. And when we could finally hold off no longer and stroked each other to urgent climaxes, the moon silvered our leaping darts of semen too.

I phoned home in the morning. Mum answered. 'I think I'll be staying the whole weekend,' I said.

'Well, thank you for telling me before I got the shopping done,' she said. 'All right, then. But be careful you don't wear out your welcome. Remember you hardly know these people yet, and they don't know you. And Bligh House...'

'Yes, I know, Mum,' I said. 'It's a far cry from Becket Street. But except for the fact they've a bit more money, they're no different from what we are.'

'Well, that's as it should be,' she said, and we ended the call. I was relieved it had gone so well.

We just wanted to spend the day together, Tom and I. Just the two of us. We didn't dare look any further ahead than that. We couldn't imagine how things were going to go on. Today, this day in late June, was all that we could see. A picture of early summer, with us in the centre of it. The sun shone from out of a cloudless sky.

When we had got out of bed Tom had dressed himself in a pair of shorts. He must have seen a look of envy on my face, because he immediately rummaged deeper in the drawer and tossed me another pair. Otherwise I'd have been in the same old jeans. Since we were exactly the same size they fitted me pretty well around the waist. But they were almost absurdly short. I think they must have been Tom's gym shorts from school, a year or two ago. They were a sort of grubby white, quite different from his khaki cargo pair. But he looked at me approvingly after I'd put them on. 'You look pretty fucking sexy in those,' he said.

We left the house taking nothing with us except a bottle of water and some sun-cream. Oh, and also our wallets, to be boringly exact. But as a major symbolic gesture we deliberately left our phones behind.

We walked up the narrow road that led along the side of Wye Down, through intermittent groves of trees, which alternated with wide open pasture. For most of the time we had the road entirely to ourselves. We tried walking each with an arm flung around the other's shoulder, once we were out of sight of Bligh House, but found that wasn't very comfortable. (Neither of us had ever experimented with that idea before.) So we went on – since there was no-one to see us looking like a pair of the the silliest sissies – holding hands. When we heard a car coming, as happened just occasionally, we simply disengaged our fingers and let our hands drop down by our sides.

There was nothing energetic or mountainous about our route. The little road made a gentle up and down climb through the Kent downs. But it ran along the south-facing scarp slope, about five hundred feet high, so that we looked out through trees that wore the fresh green of early leaf across the coast from Folkestone to Dungeness and distant Rye, with the heights of Fairlight at the limit of the view. Far out across the blue sparkling water the sun was beginning to light the white cliffs of France.

You know what I wanted to blurt out to Tom as we walked hand in hand looking down at that little lot? I think you do.

Summer was late this year, so June was giving us the hedgerow blossom-scape of May. White gauzes of Queen Anne's lace, springing gold buttercups and, in the hedges above, the scented creamy sprays of hawthorn flowers.

As we walked we spilled the secrets of our childhoods. We revealed the petty triumphs and disasters of our school-days. We talked about girls we'd used to fancy. A bit sheepishly we talked about the boys we'd fancied too. *I like you so much, Tom,* I thought. *I don't care if we're both gay, both straight, or one of each. I just can't imagine wanting to be with anybody else.* I kept getting a tight feeling in my throat, which made talking difficult at times. And from time to time that stupid pricking thing behind my eyes.

At midday we reached a village called Hastingleigh. Before we'd reached the village centre we found ourselves outside the village pub. A Georgian building perched a little way up a grassy bank beside the road. It was called The Bowl. We were two boys who enjoyed a beer or two. We didn't even need to look at each other to exchange the knowledge that we'd walked as far as we were going to go. As one, we turned our footsteps up the stepped path that led to the front door.

'You look like a pair of thirsty lads,' the landlord said. 'Been walking far?'

'From Wye,' Tom said.

'Why?' he seemed to ask.

'We just felt like a morning stroll,' Tom began, falling for the old joke I'd known for years.

'It's a joke,' I said to Tom. 'You'll get used to it.' I said to the landlord, 'He's new round here.' I ordered us a pint of Spitfire each, and picked up the snack menu.

'Live in Wye, do you?' the landlord asked.

'I do,' Tom answered. 'Why not?' Which drew a grudging laugh. 'My mate's from Chilham.'

My mate, I was now. I basked in that thought.

'Then you probably know the old story about the train,' the landlord said. We were the first customers of the day. He had no-one else to talk to. Neither did we.

'What old story about the train?' I asked. That's the protocol in this situation in a pub.

He drew enough breath to tell the tale. 'You know the local pronunciation back in the nineteenth century had Chilham and Chartham start with a hard K sound?'

'No,' I answered, 'I never knew that.'

'They used to call out on Wye station, "Kill 'em and cart 'em to Canterbury."' He laughed at his own joke.

'Why?' said Tom, poker-faced.

I nudged him in the ribs. 'Choose a fucking sandwich,' I said.

SIX

We walked back the way we had come. The afternoon sun, now facing us, turned the tree tunnels we dived in and out of into patchworks of black and gold, while the fields shone fresh green and buttercup yellow like bright pictures between the trunks.

We hadn't gone far before we both needed to pee. We stopped at a field gate to do this, looking over it and admiring the distant view of France. Actually I was also admiring another view nearer at hand. Tom had dropped his shorts halfway to his knees before letting loose his waterspout, quite knowingly, wanting to turn me on. Which of course he did. 'You tart,' I said to him. But I dropped my own shorts a similar amount, to give him a similar view, and he seemed to enjoy that too.

After zipping up we continued our progress, though by now we were both half hard. 'I suppose,' Tom said, 'I'd better tell you the story I didn't want to tell you last night.'

I chucked an arm around his shoulder for a moment, pulled his head towards me and gave him a quick peck on the cheek. 'Yes please,' I said. He'd warned me the story wasn't a very nice one. That didn't mean I wasn't keen to hear it. I was agog, actually, and so, to put it politely, was my cock.

'I've never told anyone else this,' he said as we continued along the little road. 'You'll see why. It happened at the college, my second term there.'

I did the maths. 'A little over a year ago.'

'It was the end of the afternoon. I was coming out of the toilets, passing through the locker rooms, and there were some guys there I didn't know, getting out of footie kit. They were almost naked at the moment I passed them. I must have given them a look. Well, OK, I couldn't help noticing them. They made quite a striking picture. But they caught me looking – it was really only a passing glance, but they made out it was something bigger than that. Started calling me things. Well, names don't hurt you. But then another one of them I hadn't seen came on me from behind; he'd been out of sight behind another line of lockers, I guess. He pinned my arms behind my back. Next thing they were all on me. Them nearly naked, me fully clothed.

'But I didn't stay that way for long. They started to tear my clothes off, suddenly behaving like a pack of wolves. I tried to make a joke of it. Tried to disarm them, I suppose. But once they'd pulled my trousers and pants down I knew I couldn't make a joke of it, and neither could they. My dick was as hard as it knew how to be, and it was on show to them all. They grabbed at it and teased it with their fingers. All I could do was lash out at them with my feet, my hands were tightly held behind me, but they easily dodged my kicks.

'It was like they'd scented blood. They bundled me round a corner into a space where no-one much went, where sports equipment was stored. Then, one by one, they took off what little they wearing. And guess what? They were all hard too. Fucking hypocrites they were.'

I said gently, 'You don't have to go on if you don't want to. If it hurts.' I could see that it did.

'I want to tell you,' he said determinedly. 'You're the only person I've ever wanted to tell.'

I took his hand again, and we walked on like that while he continued with his tale.

'My jeans were round my ankles, my pullover and shirt were off. They pushed me forwards over the back of a chair, my arse in the air, my cock poking through between the rungs of the chair-back. One bloke was still holding my arms, another was behind me too, and I could feel his wet cock nosing between my thighs. I was going to be raped, I thought. And OK, I was scared. Almost to the point of shitting myself.'

'Which might have put them off,' I volunteered practically.

'Somehow I don't think so,' was his grim reply. He went on, 'Another guy was crouching in front of me, in front of the chair, and wanking my cock roughly, so roughly that it really hurt, pulling the foreskin too far back. And the others stood around, shamelessly masturbating their own dicks as they watched. They went on calling me names. Pansy and so on, and worse than that, of course.

'Then suddenly I was saved. Two big guys came round the corner, and one of them yelled, really loudly, "Jesus, what the fuck are you lot doing?" The other one – I could only half see this, grabbed at the two guys who were behind me and pulled them off me, and at the same moment I shot my load all over the chair.

'There was a moment of chaos, of shouting and a few punches half-thrown. Then everybody sort of calmed down, and the blokes who'd got hold of me drifted back round the corner, scrambling into their underwear as they went. The guys who'd rescued me helped me stand up. They looked down at my wet cock and couldn't help smiling a bit at that. One asked me if I was OK. I said I was. I was glad I hadn't started to cry. He patted my naked bum. He said, "Better get dressed. And don't tangle with that lot again." Then they left me to try and put my dignity back together on my own.'

'Oh, bloody hell,' I said. I couldn't think of anything else to say. I'd been a bit knocked out by what he'd said. I was hurting for him, for what had happened to him, and what had nearly happened to him. I was also very moved by the fact that he'd chosen to share the event with me, to admit to such a shaming humiliation.

But there was another thing. Which shamed *me*. I'd got turned on by hearing his account. My cock was now very hard inside my shorts. I wanted to do to Tom what had nearly been done to him on that occasion. Though more gently, of course. And more … let's just say, affectionately.

Then, to my surprise, he laughed. 'Well, I'm glad I got that off my chest,' he said. 'And glad it was with you. But do you know what? Telling you all that – although I was reliving something really awful – has given me a boner now.' He said that last bit rather shyly.

I said, feeling equally awkward about it, 'It's done the same for me.'

We walked on a little further, though we both knew we'd want to stop soon. Things needed to be released, things that had been building up all day. In a physical sense, of course. But not only that. We were both in an emotional state that was new to us. We were moving into territory that was uncharted, as far as we were concerned: into areas of ourselves we hadn't yet explored.

'Did you cry after it was all over?' I asked him. 'I know I'd have done.' I thought I'd probably have been blubbing from the start.

'You bet I did,' he said. 'I went back into the toilet and sat there and sobbed for half an hour. Then again when I was in bed that night.' He turned and looked sideways at me. 'I may look tough and brave in public,' he said. 'But it's just a show. Except that now... Now I don't have to pretend for you.'

'Oh hey,' I said, a bit choked. Another word had nearly popped out just then, instead of hey. A word that begins with D and ends with G. I was glad I'd managed to hold it back. Stupid me.

Now I realised why that thrown away remark, *fucking little poofs,* in the doorway of the Tickled Trout last night had upset him so. He'd been called a poof and nearly been fucked – nearly been raped – last year. Talk about traumatised. Perhaps he would never want to be fucked. By me or anyone. Perhaps he'd never want to fuck me. Perhaps all we'd ever do together would be what we'd already done. Well, if that was the case, I could live with that. What was good enough for him was good enough for me. I would never now want anything that he didn't want too. And I'd be very careful with him, very careful of him. He was very precious to me at that moment, and I wanted to wrap him in cotton wool. And take him home in my pocket.

'Hey,' he said suddenly. He beckoned me sideways with mischievous eyes. There was a gate into a field. He vaulted over it. I vaulted over it too. He grabbed me and kissed me, extrovertly, confidently. At that moment at least, he didn't seem to need wrapping in cotton wool.

We didn't need prompting about what would happen next. We didn't stand on the ceremony of undressing each other the way we'd done the last two nights. We just began, without saying anything about it, to undress ourselves.

Last night the moon had lit the contours of our nakedness. Today, this afternoon, it was the sun. I don't know which of us lay on his back first and invited the other with open arms to lie on top of him. Only that, as soon as we'd done that, we did it the other way round.

We did nothing beyond that for ages. There was nothing beyond that we needed to do. Except shoot, obviously. And we knew that would happen, one way or another, in God's good time.

I'd had so little experience of sex. Every bit of it has been related here. But what was happening now was mind-blowingly new. I was rolling with a boy, a beautiful boy, a boy who had a not-very-big physique like me. We were naked in a field of grass that gave up

54

its summer scents more and more, the more we rolled on it. Clovers, daisies, vetches and trefoils. Wild thyme too. It was quite Shakespearean in its novelty and power.

I had his cock in my hand. He had mine in his. I thought – if that isn't too cold a word for the emotional processes in play at that moment – that I wasn't sure what I wanted to happen next. But then I knew. I ducked down. I pushed my head into his groin and took his prick in my mouth.

I knew from the way his body behaved that no-one had ever done this to him before. Nobody teaches you to do this. But the procedure is fairly obvious to any boy who masturbates. You move your head back and forth until the other guy comes in your mouth. It wasn't long before Tom did. The taste of it was something I couldn't have guessed at. Sour and salty. Pungent, like a rather whiffy oyster. In other circumstances I'd have thought it foul. But because it was Tom I didn't. I wolfed him down.

He held on to my head for a minute, so that I couldn't release my mouth from his cock. Or couldn't have done without a struggle. I didn't struggle. I didn't mind. Then he let me go. 'Have you come?' he asked me quietly.

'No,' I said, although my naked cock now trembled on the brink of doing so.

'Do you want me to do the same to you?'

I just nodded, beginning to sit up beside him. He pushed me gently downwards till I lay on my back among the uncut grass and flowers. Then lying alongside he bent his head in and did to me exactly what I'd done to him. I never knew anything could be so good. I was in ecstasy. Though not for long. Just seconds, probably. Then I emptied myself – poured out my whole being, it felt like – into his mouth. Without letting go of me, without changing the rhythm of his stroking head, he drank all of me.

Gradually we sat up, our legs still stretched on the grass, our erections abandoned and waning. We looked at each other searchingly, exploring each other's eyes. Looking in each other's face for clues.

Then Tom said, 'I love you, Mick.'

I said, 'I love you too.'

Silently we both began to cry.

SEVEN

'Tom, Tom, Tom. It's the only name we hear,' my father said. 'What's happened to all your other friends?'

'They're still around,' I said. And they were. It was just that I wasn't spending any time with them.

'And this Scotland trip,' my mother put in. 'Are you sure they're going to want you all that time? A whole two weeks...'

'I'll be earning my keep,' I said. 'The house is in a bit of a state, apparently. They need all the help they can find to get it straight again.'

'Then they should be paying you,' Mum said. You couldn't win with her. One minute she was worrying I'd be a burden to Tom's family, the next that I'd be a child slave. Going up chimney flues, naked, with a brush...

'It'll be fine,' I said.

'You ought to have him round here for a meal,' Mum said then, changing tack once more. 'At least we could meet him properly. Since you spend so much time with him. It'd be nice to get to know him a bit ourselves.'

'Invite him from us,' Dad said. 'Tell him he's welcome to spend the night. It's the least we can offer. Since you've been spending almost every night over there for a week and more.'

All of that was true. Since that walk across Wye Down to Hastingleigh, Tom and I had practically been living together at Bligh House. I'd spent a few odd nights at Becket Street for the sake of appearances – for the sake of my parents. But Tom and I had fallen heavily into the first rapture of first love, and ever since that first mutual avowal (there had been plenty more since, in identical terms) we were finding it almost physically painful to spend any length of time apart.

I had mixed feelings, though, about entertaining Tom at Becket Street. There's always an awkwardness when a relatively poor kid has a relatively rich one visit him, at least there is when you're in your late teens, and it's felt more keenly by the poorer one of course. But that was compounded by the nature of our new relationship. I wasn't 'out' to my parents. After all, I wasn't even out to myself. Not about being gay. I wasn't happy yet with that label for myself. Nor was Tom. All we had confronted so far was the fact that our particular situation involved the strongest love we'd felt for anyone. We hadn't yet gone from the particular to the general. We hadn't admitted to ourselves or to each other that we were a pair of poofs, that we were gay. There was just that thing we had together: that unique Tom'n'Mick thing. Tom'n'Mick. Mick'n'Tom.

Tom's parents behaved wonderfully with us. They treated it as a perfectly normal thing that their eldest son, who'd never had a girlfriend, should have latched onto a less wealthy kid from college. Latched onto him so firmly that he wanted no other company: spent his evenings in the pub with him, his weekends on long rambles alone with him in the countryside, and wanted him to share his bedroom with him night after night after night. Surely they must have guessed what was going on, I thought. They were both highly intelligent people: his mother a teacher, his father an official in one of the larger banks. They'd have to be mightily unobservant, or else very deeply in denial, not to have twigged what was going on. But assuming that they had twigged... Well, what wonderful parents they appeared to be. I very much doubted that mine would respond the same way if they realised that the rich kid they were going to invite for dinner was bedding their son.

I have to say that Mum did us proud. Dad too, in his way. There was gin and tonic to get us started, which we drank in our small garden, under the apple tree. Then we went indoors and had a sort of smoked salmon and cottage cheese parcel which Mum had found in Waitrose. A casserole of beef and red wine followed – it was something Mum always did well, sprinkling parsley over the top just as it was served, so that it looked like a bistro dish – then a crumble made of summer fruit. I might have volunteered to do the food. I was the trainee chef, after all, and Mum was not. But something told me I needed to let her run with this.

Dad did tend to interview my friends rather, whenever he met one, and he didn't make an exception in Tom's case. Where had Tom gone to school? Cranbrook. Then why hadn't he gone to a good university like Cambridge, instead of a lowly local college like...? Like mine. I wasn't very pleased at hearing that question put. If Tom hadn't done very well for himself in ending up where he was, the implication was that neither had I.

But Tom answered very sweetly, not taking umbrage, or at least not showing it if he had. He'd always wanted to do art and design, he said. Interior design was the career he'd set his heart on. An academic course at a university didn't fit with that ambition, and so that was that.

Telling my parents he wanted a career in interior design was a pretty good give-away, I thought. He might as well have told them he'd always wanted to be a hairdresser. But if they made the connection with any particular stereotype they gave no sign of it. At least not then.

When bedtime came there was no question of Tom sleeping with me. We had a perfectly good spare room – it was the room that had once been shared by my sisters – while my own room had only one small single bed in it. To have insisted on our sharing it would have been more confrontational and up-front about our relationship than either of us was yet prepared to be.

So we went off to bed in our separate rooms, after briefly kissing goodnight in the bathroom after cleaning our teeth.

In bed I couldn't sleep. The boy with whom I curled up and cuddled nightly lay in his own small bed just across the landing; my parents' bedroom lay between his room and mine. All too easily I imagined him in his small bed. Trying to get comfortable. Trying to get to sleep. Thinking about me, of course. (It wasn't vanity in me to imagine that. We knew each other very well.) I could see, feel, his fingers straying to his cock. Thinking that, of course, my own fingers strayed to mine...

A line of light appeared around the edges of my door. Then the light went out. A second later, 'Shhh, it's me.' Tom was in my room. I pulled the duvet down and he climbed in with me. I was naked. He was, for reasons of prudence, in his dressing-gown. It took us a moment or two to wriggle him out of that.

'I fancied a wank,' he whispered, a laugh in his voice at the same time. A laugh that's a whisper, talking about wanking; it's quite sexy, that; you probably know. 'You going to help me out?'

Yes, I was going to. Yes, I did. The danger that we'd waken my parents with our thrashings about, and with the bed creaking, added spice to the event. After we'd both come we cuddled and kissed for about a quarter of an hour, I suppose. Not that I looked at my watch. Perversely we enjoyed the growing discomfort of our cooling wetness. Then Tom said, 'I'll have to go. Dream of me. Dream only of me. See you in the morning.' He slid out of the bed, slipped his dressing-gown back on and disappeared through the door.

I listened with ears honed sharply as an owl's as his soft footfall crossed the landing and he let himself back into his own room. I listened to the silence that followed. I lay back with a feeling of the utmost relief. We'd got away with it, I thought.

We had to be up early in the morning: it was a college day, and Dad had to go off to work too. We breakfasted together, the four of us, on Cornflakes and toast and marmalade. Then Dad drove off. Tom and I said we'd wash up the breakfast plates. Unlike at Bligh House we didn't have a dish-washing machine at Becket Street. But Mum wouldn't hear of it. There was almost nothing to do. Tom and I should just relax during the last five minutes before we headed out to get the bus. This was very nice of her, but unfortunate, as it turned out.

What would we do with those five minutes? We'd shaved and crapped and cleaned our teeth; our backpacks were backpacked. I led the way into the living-room and sat down on the sofa, for once not giving a thought to what Tom would do. What he did do surprised me, and yet didn't surprise me, at the same time. Unfortunately the surprise it gave my mother was of a different kind.

No sooner had I settled back in my sofa seat than Tom sprang upon me. He straddled my legs, wrapped his arms about the back of my head and smackingly kissed my lips.

My mother walked in at that moment. She held in her hands the nice glasses in which we'd drunk our breakfast orange juice, and was on the way to return them to their place in the sideboard. I give her credit for not dropping them. 'Well, really,' she said. With commendable sang-froid she fiddled those glasses back into their accustomed places on the shelves, then walked back into the kitchen again.

Tom and I managed the situation less splendidly. Tom sprang backwards off me – the second time he'd done that in response to a surprise materialisation of my mum. He turned the kind of crimson colour that in a person three times his age would have presaged a stroke. I could feel that I'd done the same. We looked at each other bug-eyed with horror. We heard my mother's voice from the kitchen. 'Time you went for that bus, isn't it?' It certainly was.

We sat soberly together on the bus, wondering what the implications of my mother's surprise entry into the living-room would be. Whatever Tom's parents might or might not think about what was going on between us, we hadn't actually kissed in front of them. They hadn't even seen us holding hands. We were halfway to Canterbury before either of us spoke. Tom. 'Shit, man, I'm so sorry about that. What a fucking idiot I am.'

'No you're not,' I said. 'They're all going to find out some time soon. Maybe it's going to be uncomfortable for us when they do. Never too soon to get in practice for whatever's going to come.'

'Not many crumbs of comfort in that,' he said.

I found a way to comfort him. I wormed my hand into the side pocket of his jeans, and found the hole at the bottom of it. My fingers grasped his cock. It was soft and very small. I didn't care. I just held onto it the way I'd used to suck my thumb or held onto Bugsy the bear. After a few seconds I felt Tom's hand enter my pocket, and wriggle its way down till his fingers met and grasped my dick too. It was as shocked and shrunk as his was. Neither of us cared. We held on to each other in the secrecy of our jeans, while passengers came and went along the gangway at our side. We didn't talk, or even look at each other very much. We didn't disentangle our fingers from each other's shell-shocked prick until we arrived at the bus station in Canterbury and we had to stand up to get off the bus.

Mum said nothing to me about what she'd seen that morning. I saw her that evening, when I went home briefly, before Tom picked me up to take me to dinner at Bligh House. To take me to the Tickled Trout after that. To take me, after that, to bed. But she'd told Dad what she'd seen. He didn't say anything. But I knew from the way he looked at me that evening that he knew.

'Well, what's he going to do?' Tom said, as we sat on the riverside lawn at the Trout that night, supping wisdom-inducing pints of ale. 'Give you an earful? Wouldn't be pleasant. But you're a big boy. Take it. Give it back.' He shrugged. 'Easy to say, I know. I haven't had to do it. Yet.'

'You won't have to,' I said. 'Your folk are cool with us.'

'We'll see,' he said. I wondered for the first time if he was as anxious about his own parents' response to what was happening between us as I was about mine.

'He could turn me out of the house,' I said. Then, melodramatically, because we were on our second pint, 'They could disinherit me.'

Tom laughed. Not unkindly. 'If they throw you out – which they won't – you just come and live with me at Bligh House.' Involuntarily I raised my eyebrows. I didn't know how he'd square that with his parents. 'And if they disinherit you...' He realised he was treading on sensitive ground, and frowned his hesitation. 'Well, what have you got to lose?' It was the first time he'd referred to the disparity between our financial backgrounds. 'A house in Becket Street?'

'Not even that,' I said. 'We rent.'

'Well there you are,' he said.

But my anxiety about my own parents had overspilled into anxiety about his. 'Are you sure it's still OK about this Scotland thing?' I said. It was only three days away. The swans and their flotilla of cygnets appeared in front of us just then, sliding out of nowhere between clumps of reeds.

'Of course it is. Don't worry. I'll look after you, kid.'

He'd never called me kid before. No-one had. No-one had said they'd look after me before. My parents had done it, of course, had looked after me uncomplainingly for nineteen years, but they'd never put it into words.

I looked at him. He was as much a kid as I was. Sitting on the grass of the riverbank he looked as fragile and unsure of himself as me. I'd thought of myself as a bit of seaweed looking for a rock to anchor itself upon. But there was he, I now realised, in the same vulnerable state as I was. And still, he had promised to protect me. Did that make the offer less valuable? No way. His vulnerability, his not yet admitted fear of the consequences of what we were doing, enhanced his gesture. What he'd just said to me, *Don't worry. I'll look after you, kid,* was the most wonderful thing that had ever been said to me by anyone in the world.

EIGHT

When you do something quite mundane like catching a train with the person you're in love with, it's like doing it for the first time ever, all over again. Which meant that everything about that journey to Scotland was magically new.

It started the day before we went to Scotland actually. Tom's parents went up a day before us, in the car. That left us in charge of Bligh House for a day and night, to hand the place over to a woman neighbour who would be looking in daily to see to the cats and water the plants. We spent our night of freedom at Bligh House in some style. Getting ready for Scotland, we told each other. After the pub we sat out in the garden with a glass of whisky each and, with no-one to see us, no clothes on except a T-shirt each. Every so often one of us would get hard and we'd laugh at that. Eventually the night breeze began to chill and we romped into the house, and up to bed. There, with nobody to overhear us, we made love noisily, for the first time indulging in climactic whoops and yells.

Next day, the journey. I hadn't even had to pay my fare. Tom's dad had booked tickets for us both in advance – something my own parents had complex feelings about, of course.

How do you sit on a train with the person you've just fallen in love with. Side by side, like on the bus? Facing each other, looking into each other's eyes? But then not experiencing the same view of the countryside flashing by: one of you watches it advancing on you, the other sees it in retreat. Never mind. The question was answered for us by the position of the passengers already on the train. We sat thigh by thigh.

Starting out for Scotland from Wye is a bit odd. You set off heading south, which as everybody knows is the wrong direction. After Ashford the train at least turns west, but there's no north in the route until you get to Tonbridge, halfway to London. Only after that do you begin to feel you're on the way.

Another new thing was London itself. London-together, I mean. London Mick'n'Tom. The underground. A sandwich from Upper Crust at Kings Cross. Things we'd both experienced many times before, yet now with a sheen of novelty that made those ordinary things as extraordinary, as unreal yet as hyper-real, as if we'd been walking on the moon.

Actually, although Tom had been to Scotland before, and knew the house we were going to, I had not. Family holidays had always taken us south – to France or the Med. So that once we'd left the London suburbs behind the journey was a new one for me in real as well as emotional terms.

It took most of the day to get to Edinburgh. A brief view there of Holyrood Palace as our train braked, and an eye-popping one of Castle Rock as we slid to a stop. Later, getting off another train, we were met at Kirkaldy station by Tom's dad. He drove us out along the coast. 'That's the place,' Tom said eventually, pointing across a small inlet that was full of anchored, bobbing sailing boats. 'That's Murches.'

'The big one?' I'd seen pictures of the house already, but they hadn't prepared me for the sheer size of it. Murches looked big enough for a hotel. It stood on the edge of the shore inside a small fishing harbour, surrounded by a hamlet of small houses and what looked like a pub. The house looked very Scottish, I thought. All high pointed gables, roofed with dark slate. Lots of big sash windows facing the sea. It didn't look exactly cosy, but it was certainly impressive. It occurred to me at that moment that this place might well belong to Tom himself one day. It was a big thought, that. I turned it over in my mind, wondering what to do with it. I wondered why I hadn't had the thought before.

I hadn't given a thought to our sleeping arrangements either, and again I didn't know why. Perhaps the newness of the whole experience was so overwhelming I was responding by drifting through it, taking each new thing as it came. But when Tom's mum showed us upstairs to the room we were going to share, 'I thought you'd like to be together,' she said, without any hint of archness.

Without comment we went into the room. It was big, which was no surprise. We were more curious about the layout of the beds. There were two. One a very large double, the other a small single.

'Does she know?' I asked, as we dumped our bags on the floor.

'If you mean, have I told her, the answer's no,' said Tom. 'But I honestly don't know whether she knows or not. I do know which bed I'm having, though. The little one's yours.'

I delivered a mock-punch to his stomach, then we fell together onto the double bed, rolling around on it, laughing, in each other's arms. All the more energetically for the fact that we'd been unable to do that for the whole of the long day, prevented by the unwritten etiquette of travel on public trains.

There was fresh-caught wild salmon for dinner, with two bottles of Chablis. Afterwards no-one challenged us or asked where we were going when Tom and I headed out to have a walk around the curving beach and the harbour. We stayed out till late. At that time of year the Scottish sun barely goes down at night. We talked of random things. What they were didn't seem to matter. We were just happy to be together, me with Tom, Tom with me. At one moment we found ourselves imprudently close to the waves breaking against the harbour mole. One plume of spray splashed us and, because I was talking, a little speck of it landed on my tongue. Salty, like an oyster landing there. I'll never forget that. That evening I felt happier than I could remember feeling before – even during the wonderful three weeks I'd lived since meeting Tom. I'd never felt more alive.

I'd come prepared to earn my keep. So it was neither a disappointment nor a surprise that the next morning found Tom and me attacking the peeling paintwork of the front porch with scrapers and a blow-torch. Tom's dad thought I might not know how to use a blow-torch and would need instructing. I answered that putting the glazed caps on crème brûlées had been a good training for the morning's task. He laughed and walked away, letting us get on with the job. Even though the next couple of hours of scraping and sand-papering did bring us both out in a sweat, it was no hardship to work shoulder to shoulder with Tom. I'd willingly have swept the courtyard with a toothbrush if he had been with me doing it too.

Actually we family members (almost without thinking I find I've included myself here) weren't going to tackle all the structural problems of the house. There was a lot of stuff that needed doing by professionals. Some of the roof gullies leaked and would need their flashings renewed. In places there was plastering to be done. Tom and I and the rest of his family would in fact just be tinkering at the edges, doing the unskilled stuff. Saving a little bit of money in the process, though, which seemed sensible enough.

At work on the house today was a professional carpenter. He was tackling a couple of rotten window-sills, just a few yards away from us along the house-front. As the morning passed we grew friendly enough to call to each other from time to time, exchanging a little banter, or some comment on our respective tasks. I took more notice of him than I'd normally have done – and I noticed that Tom did too – because he was more than a bit of a dish.

He was about thirty, I reckoned. I'd never thought of myself as attracted to men of such an advanced age before. But his physical appearance at any rate was rather special. His name was Kyle. He was wearing shorts and a T-shirt. Nothing else except trainers. He sported a pair of muscular bronzed forearms and a pair of muscular bronzed legs. Tom and I, just as scantily clad, looked undeveloped in comparison. As well as pale. Kyle had red-brown hair and, an unusual accompaniment to that, flashing blue eyes. He had a small snub nose and an uncomplicated smile. I, who wasn't sure if I fancied men as a general rule or only Tom – and certainly had never thought I might fancy a thirty-year-old – was suddenly forced to confront the fact that I fancied Kyle.

I didn't tell Tom that.

In the afternoon Tom and I were released from our labours. We were going to knock around, lie around, on the beach. I popped upstairs quickly to get some sun-cream for us both.

Kyle had brought another carpenter to work with him for the afternoon. His partner or assistant, I wasn't sure which. I took little notice of him when he arrived. A thin young man with straight dark hair, he was less obviously attractive than Kyle at a first glance. Now as I emerged from our bedroom I heard voices below. I peered over the banister rail. At the bottom of the stairwell, in the rather watery light coming down from the skylight above me Kyle was giving some instructions to his mate – who was called David – about his tasks for the afternoon. And then I saw something that stopped me short. Kyle finished giving his orders and, as he stopped speaking, reached round David's back and patted him on the bum. But that wasn't all. David responded by leaning in to Kyle, angling his head up a little – he was s little smaller than Kyle was – and kissing him quickly on the lips. There followed another blink-and-you-miss-it mutual pat on bums, and then the two men turned away from each other, to continue their work on different parts of the house.

I waited some time before descending the stairs. I didn't want Kyle or David to know I'd seen what I just had. Whatever that was.

I met Tom just outside the front door. By now Kyle was set up at a temporary workbench made from a plank on trestles, cutting fillets of wood to length just a few feet away. Tom said to Kyle as we prepared to walk away, 'Just off to the beach for a bit.'

Kyle laughingly replied, 'All right for some.'

I hadn't had time to make sense of what I'd seen him and David do. Let alone ask Tom what his interpretation of it might be. My brain was in a whirl. So that the next thing I did, I did spontaneously, without pausing for thought. I drew Tom's head towards mine as we started to walk away and, still in full view of Kyle – though no-one else – gave him a peck on the cheek.

'What the fuck are you doing?' Tom hissed in my ear. He'd gone almost rigid with anger, or else shock.

'It's OK,' I whispered back urgently. 'Walk on. I'll explain.' As soon as we were out of sight and out of earshot I told Tom what I'd witnessed from the stairs.

'It could have meant anything,' Tom said. 'You can't assume anything. We've hardly arrived here and you've kissed me in public, right in Kyle's face. At least he had the good sense to kiss David privately – if that was what he was doing, and we can't even be sure of that – rather than in full view on the seafront.'

'I just went with my instinct,' I said. 'It seemed the right thing to do. If I called it wrong, then I'm sorry.'

'If you got it wrong we'll both be sorry. A tiny village like this. It could be all over the pub by tonight that the newest arrivals in the village are a couple of...' He tailed off. He didn't even want to choose a word for us. We were having our first ever – first ever – disagreement, Tom and I. And, oh God, did it hurt!

It was if a cloud had crossed the sun, for both of us. We went down to the beach and mucked about, and lay in the sun. We talked about other things. No rancour. We were still friends and we laughed together and we were still in love. But that moment of tension between us had hurt us somehow, in a way that we couldn't, and didn't try to, explain. All our time together up to now had been perfect. In a way that I had never dreamt anything could be perfect. On the bus. In the bed. Walking to Hastingleigh. Travelling by train. Stripping paint... Not even the overheard remark of *fucking little poofs* in the doorway of the Tickled Trout had ever put a damper on things between us. But now this had. My stupid kiss and Tom's reaction to it. It lay like a faintly soiled veil across the beauty of the afternoon. At several points I felt myself wanting to cry. And once I looked at Tom's face and saw, or thought I saw, that he was struggling with the same thing.

As luck would have it our return towards Murches coincided with Kyle and David's clocking off and going home. We met them walking along the shore towards us. As we drew close I saw a broad grin break out on Kyle's face, and a shy smile on David's. I wondered if either of them would say anything. Kyle did.

'You lads been in the Stewart Arms yet?' That was the name of the so far unexplored village pub. 'David and me'll be popping in there early doors tonight. Round six o'clock. If you fancied joining us for a quick one … well, it'd be great to see you.' This was said in such an open and friendly way that even Tom was completely disarmed.

'Hey, yes,' he said. I could hear relief and delight together in his voice. 'Be really great.' We passed on, and said no more as our paths crossed and took us out of sight. Then Tom said to me, 'I'm sorry I doubted you. Sorry I spoke the way I did. Your instinct was right.'

'You were right to tell me off. I should have been more careful.' I felt a great wave of something welling up inside me, but resisted the urge to throw my arms around Tom right there and then. We went indoors and ran upstairs into our room. We threw each other together onto the bed, hugged and kissed, and cried unstoppably down each other's cheeks in the way that lovers do, for no particular reason other than the overwhelming confusion of happiness.

NINE

We got there first. Tom ordered two pints of Belhaven. I was glad he knew the right thing to say. I'd have asked for bitter, and would have been served my beer politely, but then been left with the feeling that I'd crossed the Scottish border without doing the proper research.

Then I realised we hadn't got there first. It was quite dark inside the Stewart Arms. Only now did we realise Kyle and David were watching us, pints of beer in hand, from a table at the end of the room. For a second I thought the worst of them. They hadn't wanted to show themselves until we'd already bought our first drinks, to avoid having to dig into their own pockets.

A moment later, once we'd walked over to join them, and seen how shy but genuine their smiles of welcome were, I realised my mistake with shame. Their failure to come forward sooner sprang not from lack of generosity but from something else. I saw them suddenly as they must have seen themselves. Two gay men of thirty who had asked two teenagers to meet them in a pub and were now wondering if they'd been over-forward, or if one of them had misinterpreted a half-glimpsed kiss.

It went well from then on. Thanks to Kyle, who took a brave leap as soon as we'd sat down with them. 'So how long have you two been together?' he asked.

To my great surprise, Tom, as un-ready up to now as I was to acknowledge that we were a gay couple or anything of the sort, said coolly, 'Three weeks. And you two?'

They looked at each other, which I thought was sweet. 'Lived together for three years now,' said David, who hadn't spoken till then. 'Worked together for six.'

'We were at school together,' Kyle said.

'Well, not exactly,' David objected. 'He was five years ahead.'

'I only meant we were at school at the same time,' Kyle clarified with a smile. 'Not that I deflowered you when you were a kid.'

I was in admiration of the way they could deal with different nuances in the way they saw things. Defusing potential conflict with a smile, a joke. It was like an object lesson in how a couple – a gay couple, I have to use the expression from now on – could operate. The first gay couple that Tom and I had met up close. Were we looking at ourselves ten years down the line? It wasn't a bad picture if we were.

I heard Tom say, 'Do your parents know? I mean, they must. How did you tell them?' I'd thought it was only me who was worried about telling his parents and how they would react. I'd thought that Tom was cool about it with his mum and dad. I realised now that he had the same anxiety I did. He hadn't volunteered that to me. Had I told him my own worries on that score? No. In the company of Kyle and David things were beginning to come out.

Kyle and David looked at each other before answering. Then it was Kyle, older than David by five years, who spoke first. They both seemed to find it natural that he would take the lead. 'Mine guessed when I was younger,' was what Kyle said. 'I didn't need to come out to them. My dad took me out for a drink when I was about twenty or twenty-one. He told me that if I was gay – *if* I was – he and Mum would have no problem with it. He didn't want me to say anything in reply. I didn't need to volunteer anything I didn't want to, he told me, but he and Mum would always be there for me if I wanted to talk. That was the end of the conversation. I found it embarrassing at the time, and so did my dad. We were glad to move on and talk about other things. But afterwards I was bloody relieved the conversation happened, and that Dad had said what he did. When David and I moved in together I just told them so and they took it without fuss and wished us luck. They both liked David anyway, and now they like it when I bring him round to their place.' He looked at David. 'I've been lucky, I guess.'

'It's been a bit different for me,' David said, an awkward half smile hovering on his lips. 'My parents are a bit churchy, if you know what I mean. I kind of figured that they wouldn't want to know I was gay. That they'd have a terrible problem with it. So I haven't actually come out to them yet.'

'So what happened when you moved in with Kyle?' I asked. I was excited, awed by the situation I found myself in. Here were Tom and I, meeting a real live gay couple for the first time, and talking matily over pints of beer about the issues involved in being … well, a gay couple. There, I'd thought the words at last.

David looked uncomfortable with my question but he answered it gamely. 'I told them I was moving out – out from their house, I mean – and going to share a cottage with Kyle, my business partner, who they already knew. It's just a cheap little place,' David ran on nervously now. 'Nothing grand. We rent it from...'

Kyle stopped him. 'That's not what Mick was asking about,' he told David gently and, not caring whether anyone else in the bar saw him or not, patted him on the knee.

David returned to the point. 'It's been a bit like, don't ask, don't tell. I think they kind of know but don't want to know at the same time. They know Kyle and they're OK with him. In a way they're happier to think I'm sharing a home with a male friend than they would be if I was living with a girl out of wedlock. I told you they're a bit strict on the religious front. Only I don't think they would be so happy if they knew, or thought, that Kyle and I actually had sex.'

'So what do they think you do?' Tom asked. Before today I couldn't have imagined Tom asking such a question. Not even asking it of himself, let alone putting it to someone six years older than himself.

'I don't know,' said David. 'They like to keep their heads in the sand, I think.'

Something obvious struck me. 'You haven't gone for a civil partnership, then?'

They looked at each other. Then Kyle turned back to me and spoke. 'Not yet. Maybe we can't while David's parents are alive. Who knows?' He shrugged.

I took heed of that. Here were two young men, openly gay, and able to touch each other lightly in the village pub without causing a stir (it helped that Kyle at least was a big, muscular type, I think) but unable to go the final mile because of what one of them's parents might think.

Kyle said, and it was like he was tuning into my own thought process, 'Nothing in life is perfect. No relationship can be perfect. But you have to take what you've got, and make that as nearly perfect as you can. Then you'll be all right.' Then he put his hand into the pocket of his cargo shorts and pulled out a wallet. 'I'm going to get you boys another pint.'

I couldn't help thinking that Tom might be as lucky in his parents as Kyle had been with his. Whereas I was possibly going to experience the same ongoing difficulty with mine as David obviously had with his.

When Kyle came back with four fresh pints – actually he didn't carry them all, I'd got up and helped him bring them – Tom blurted out another question that startled me. He was doing a lot of that this evening. 'If you love someone of your own sex very much, does it mean you're gay?'

Both Kyle and David looked surprised by the question, unsure what to say. Then Kyle spoke. 'You're talking about yourself and Mick, is that right?' he asked carefully.

'Yes,' said Tom staunchly.

'That's an amazing thing to say publicly,' Kyle said. 'To people you don't know very well yet. In a pub. You probably don't realise what you've just done.' He looked at David. 'I don't think we've ever had the balls to do that.'

David appeared to take this as a criticism of himself. 'Then I'll fucking do it now,' he said. He turned to Tom and me. 'Kyle and I love each other totally. Without condition.' He looked back to Kyle. 'That OK?'

'Oh hey,' said Kyle. He laughed a bit, but was clearly touched more deeply than he knew how to express. I realised we had just witnessed a big moment between the two of them. Then Kyle returned his attention to Tom and his question. 'What is gay? Gay's just a three-letter word. Poof's a four-letter one.'

'Queer has five,' volunteered David.

'Faggot has six,' I said, quickly getting the hang of this.

'They're all just words,' Kyle said. 'Words that don't mean very much. Love's a word that does mean something. Means everything, in a way. There's nothing more to it than that.' He raised his pint glass. 'Cheers, guys,' he said.

We realised we'd have to leave when we'd finished our second pint. We were expected back for dinner at Murches. Tom's mother was roasting a chicken for us, and it would have been very rude to cry off. Yet we both wanted to spend longer with Kyle and David. The first kindred spirits we'd ever met. It was like finding our gurus, if you like. There was so much we wanted to learn from them. So much we wanted to know about.

They were quick to sense this. 'We must spend some more time together, while you're up here,' Kyle announced. Then suddenly there was a look on his face that showed he thought he'd been too forward again, that he was imposing the company of two older men on two kids who might not want it very much.

We were quick to reassure him. 'That'd be great,' Tom said. 'I'd really like to stay and talk to you – listen to you – all night. Get pissed. It's just that...' He explained, rather unnecessarily, about the dinner that was being cooked.

'Tell them about the boat on Saturday,' David said to Kyle.

'They won't want to come on that,' Kyle told him.

'What boat?' I asked. 'Why not want to come out on a boat?' The bay bobbed with boats. Fishing boats, sailing boats. I'd never been on a boat. I'd always longed to, truth be told.

'It's not what you might think,' Kyle said to me. 'There's a sailing race in the bay this Saturday. But we're not taking part. What we're doing isn't all that interesting. David and I are simply manning the race control boat. Starting the race, and clocking the finishing times. Do a spot of fishing in between. Nothing more exciting than that.'

It sounded exciting enough to me. 'Can we come with you?' I heard myself almost beg. 'I'd love to do that. Tom, wouldn't you?' I almost felt myself welling up.

'Oh hey, I'd love that,' said Tom. Much to my relief. 'Could we join you?' A thought hit him. 'Oh no. We're probably not allowed...'

'Of course you are,' said Kyle. 'It's just that you might find it a bit tame. If you've done proper sailing, that is.'

'I've never done proper sailing,' I said. I'd never been on the sea, except the ferry once or twice to France. 'Never been out in a small boat.'

I must have sounded really pathetic. Kyle gave me an odd look. Then he looked at Tom and saw the same beseeching look on his face. Then he turned to David. 'Blimey,' he said, 'I never knew youngsters could be so easily pleased. You weren't, at their age.' He turned back to Tom and me. 'Saturday it is, then. You're on.' He sounded really chuffed.

We lay in our double bed later, side by side, gently playing with each other's cock. The bed's very doubleness was still a novelty, still a wonder, on this our second night. Even 'side by side' was a new position for us – in bed at any rate. We talked about the day we'd had. I praised Tom's mother's cooking (the roast chicken, with lemon, garlic and tarragon had been superb) and we remembered together the after dinner walk we'd taken, this second night, again along the beach. We'd gone to the far end of the harbour arm and there even Tom had felt confident enough, and distant enough from the eyes of the village, to give me a long hard snog.

That confidence had come from our meeting with Kyle and David in the pub and the things they'd talked us through. Also from the things they hadn't said, but had taught us just by being there. Just by being themselves.

Absently, playfully, Tom pulled my foreskin back. 'What do you think those two are doing now?' he asked.

'The same as us,' I suggested.

'They might be fast asleep, on the other hand,' Tom said. 'We don't know how much they had to drink after we left them. And anyway, they have to get up early in the morning. They'll be here at work in the morning while we...'

'Are still tucked up here, doing this again,' I said. 'Lucky us,' I added, in what I hoped would pass for a philosophical tone.

'Or lucky them,' said Tom, in what really was a philosophical tone.

'Getting up at sparrow's crack to start work...?'

'OK,' said Tom. 'Why not? They're not rich, they have to work all hours, but they've got each other and they know exactly who they are. Isn't that the best thing of all?'

He sounded so serious that I actually stopped stroking his dick for a second. 'I guess it is.' I pondered my own answer for a moment. 'I'd like to be like them in ten years' time,' I said.

Tom's reply was the best possible. He rolled around towards me, engulfed my whole body in a muscular squeeze and said, 'That's what I wanted you to say. You've made me happy saying that. I've been thinking all evening – that's what I want too.'

'They might, of course, have decided not to care about getting to sleep,' I said, mischievous all of a sudden. 'Not to care about having to get up early. Let the morning take care of itself. Right now they may be having a bloody good fuck.'

'In which case,' Tom answered with a hint of laughter in his voice, 'which one of them is fucking who?'

'Whom,' I corrected jokingly, grabbing his cock and starting to stroke it again. I was glad Tom found himself able to talk lightly now, for the first time, about a subject that was difficult for him. 'You'll have to ask them that yourself. Probably the kind of question that'll surface naturally when we're on a boat with them a couple of miles out to sea.'

'Roll on Saturday,' said Tom.

Anthony McDonald

TEN

Tom's mum asked me if – since I was a student at catering college – I'd like to cook dinner for them one night. I didn't have to say yes if I thought it would be a hassle. Only if I felt I'd really like to. I said, of course I'd like to. It would be an honour. I'd do it that night. I suggested a seasonal French one-pot stew. How did that sound? There was a farmers' market in the village that day. I would go and get the ingredients right away.

'Take my purse,' said Tom's mum. If I were to have a mother-in-law, then Tom's mum would be my first choice, I thought.

I left poor Tom still scraping away at the pilasters of the portico. I wouldn't be long, I told him. Anyway, he had Kyle for company again this morning: he was expertly chopping rotten sections out of window-sills with a chisel a few yards away. There'd been no sign of David yet.

That changed when I got into the village centre. As I walked towards the farmers' market, I almost ran into David as he came out of the doorway of a shop. We said good morning and stopped for a moment to chat. Then I asked him a question that, since my conversation in bed with Tom last night, I wanted the answer to, and I was glad of the chance to put it to David when he was alone. 'Where can you buy condoms round here?'

David didn't laugh, or look at me with any surprise, for which I gave inward thanks. 'The best place would be Boots in Kircaldy.' Eight miles, a car ride, away. 'There's a machine in the gents' by the harbour jetty, but it often runs out. You can't depend on it.' He must have seen a look of disappointment or anxiety on my face because he then said, 'Look, we've got loads at home. I'll bring you a supply to be going on with. When do you want them by?' He must have heard how cheeky or else ridiculous his question had sounded even as he asked it. His face crumpled into a smile and he giggled. 'Perhaps that wasn't very tactful,' he said.

'No rush,' I said. 'Probably not for another couple of days.'

David laughed, very sweetly. 'I won't even think of asking why.' We went on our separate ways.

I got lamb shoulder, which I would dice. Then baby new potatoes, big spring onions and shallots, baby turnips and carrots. Then broad beans, new peas and courgettes. A bottle of V8 vegetable juice and a bottle of cheap white wine. Then I went back to Murches along the beach. I wouldn't need to start preparing the meal till much later in the day. I joined Tom at his labours in the porch. By now David was working alongside Kyle a few feet away. He turned and gave me a wink when I arrived. I said nothing about condoms to Tom.

The stew is called a navarin of lamb, or *navarin printanier*. Spring lamb and turnip stew is a rough translation. The secret lies in having very small veg – especially the turnips and potatoes, of as nearly as possibly equal size. You sear the lamb cubes in olive oil, then add the vegetable juice and white wine. Pop it in a steady oven for an hour. Add all the root vegetables and shallots and cook for another half hour. Then in go the broad beans, cubed courgettes and peas. Fifteen more minutes, then quickly stir in lumps of mashed butter and flour to thicken the gravy.

I served it on big plates, sprinkled with parsley, and with a salad by its side. Everyone said how splendid it was. Privately I thought so too. I'd never made it before. For afters I'd done a chilled summer pudding of red fruits, served with clotted cream. We were just finishing this, with a glass of Beaujolais (it goes better with summer fruits than any white wine) when there was a knock at the dining-room door and David astonishingly poked his head around it. 'Sorry,' he said, 'but I have an urgent delivery for Mick.'

I got up from the table, feeling that my face had flushed the colour of the summer fruit and the Beaujolais, and relieved David of the burden he was carrying in a (mercifully folded-over) supermarket bag. I rushed up to the bedroom with it and stowed it away. Then I rushed back downstairs again and rejoined the family at the table. 'What the hell was all that about?' Tom whispered across to me.

'Never you mind,' I whispered back.

To my surprise Tom forgot about the mysterious parcel and the equally mysterious appearance of David in the dining-room, and the rest of his family were simply too well-brought up to mention it. In the case of Tom, though, it was probably because we had better things to think and talk about after dinner, and even better things to do. Soon I'd forgotten the incident also.

'You're a fucking star, mate,' Tom said as soon as we'd left the house for our nightly ramble along the shore. 'Cooking like that. You really wowed my mum and dad. I hope you saw their faces. Jesus, I'm so proud of you!'

'Oh hey,' I said, a bit overcome. I hadn't expected a reaction quite as strong as that, even from Tom.

'You know what,' he went on as we ambled among the boats along the quay. 'You can cook for me for the rest of my life.'

'I fully intend to,' I said. And then I stopped. Tom stopped too. We'd both spoken flippantly. But it was as if we'd each, without thinking, tossed a pebble into a rock-pool and had suddenly disturbed all the currents and the wildlife there. There was a silence. Which at last I broke. I heard my voice sound as fragile as it had ever done, even when I was child. 'I meant that,' I said.

'So did I,' said Tom. He'd had time to compose himself better than I'd done. He put an arm around my shoulder as we walked on, heedless of whether we were observed or not. His arm felt so strong. And I, just six months younger than him, felt suddenly, stupidly, like a child.

We came to the point where Kyle and David's boat was moored. We didn't go down the ladder and try to board it, though we could have done easily enough. Our invitation was for tomorrow, not tonight. We just stood looking down at it as it lay below us on the low tide. It was a stocky, butch little pilot launch, with a small upright control cabin, on top of which was mounted an impressive amount of radar, radio and safety equipment, though it had no sail. It had been the harbour master's patrol vessel until last year, Kyle had told us. The harbour master had moved on and got himself a more high-tech affair, selling the cast-off to David and Kyle. 'All set for tomorrow?' Tom said, turning to me. Then, 'Let's go down onto the beach.'

I kind of guessed what that meant, and so Tom's suggestion excited me. A minute after we'd disappeared from the view of any but the most determined of prying eyes, Tom pulled me down onto a rock, undid and then lowered my shorts and sucked me off. He was getting better at this day by day. So was I. Without bothering to pull my shorts back up I then repaid Tom's compliment. When I'd finished, I stood up, wiping my lips with the back of my hand. Tom said, with a chuckle, 'So what's left to do when we get to bed?'

'I'm sure we'll think of something,' I said.

It was one of those beautiful mornings when the world looks so magical it seems to have turned into a star. The sea danced blue and diamond, and the land smelled of summer. We met Kyle and David at the top of the ladder that descended to their boat, as we'd arranged. The only surprise was that they'd brought someone else along. A kid of eleven. 'My nephew,' Kyle introduced the boy. 'Orlando.' I thought it was rather a splendid name. I also thought Orlando was a rather splendid looking boy.

In addition to Orlando, Kyle had brought big sea-fishing rods, and a back-pack that contained a weighty collection of cans of beer. We all swung down the ladder like a pack of marmosets and then Kyle started the engine and David, still in monkey mode, cast off the mooring ties. I found myself thinking the thought that seems to be shared by all boys, regardless of whether they're straight or gay. That life moves onto a more heavenly plane if you're granted some time out with a boat, a fishing rod and a few cans of beer.

How quickly the shore receded and became somewhere else, its complex of wharves and jetties, ladders and chains disappearing below the line of the seafront walk and the houses along it, from among which Murches soon rose majestically into view. And then Murches was dwarfed, and the village in its turn was dwarfed, within a minute or two, by the hills behind. All was reduced to its essentials: Scotland, a long wavy line between us and sky; and the here, the now, the sea.

I must have been in a kind of day-dream watching this. Because I was startled to hear Orlando's young voice close by my ear, saying, 'Want a beer?' He was fishing a can out of the backpack before I'd got my answer out. (It was yes, I need hardly say.) Orlando wasn't allowed to share the beer, of course. It was ginger beer for him, but he seemed more than happy enough with that. Like us, he was excited by the magic of the waves, the heady salty buffet of the sea.

We went through the drill we would have to follow when we started the race in a few minutes' time. We would anchor near a yellow marker buoy. Five minutes before the start David, who was the timekeeper, would call five, and I would raise a special flag as high as I could. When David called four, a minute after that, Tom would raise a differently marked flag. Then when the time came, Orlando would blow the starting horn with all his might, and both flags would be whacked down. Kyle meanwhile would use the engines and steering gear to keep the boat from drifting too much or dragging its anchor chain.

It all worked like clockwork. There was something surreal, I thought, about landlubbers Tom and me waving flags to an array of bells-and-whistles sailing boats, while an eleven-year-old boy started the proceedings with a blast on his elf-sized horn, like Pan. The boats, till then milling around us on the nervy swell, then charged off on their figure-of-eight course around the bay.

And then we lowered our rods over the side and waited for the fish to show up.

'You know what?' Kyle said, as Orlando handed round the second course of beer. 'When you're back in England you two should think about getting a place together of your own. A flat in Canterbury or something. Since you're both at college there.' Canterbury seemed just then a terribly long way away. An irrelevant place. Just as the future was in irrelevant time.

'That'll cost them a bit, though,' Orlando put in surprisingly. He seemed rather wise for his years.

'Money's not the only thing,' Kyle told him. 'There's things like freedom and independence. Like with David and me. Just wait a few years, Orlando. You'll soon see.'

'Talk about a place of your own, though,' David said a bit dreamily. 'Tom's got Murches to look forward to one day.'

'Oh come on,' Kyle objected good-humouredly. 'That's running ahead a bit. He's got to wait for his parents to die before that happens. And I'm sure that's not at the forefront of his mind just now. At least I hope it's not.'

'I only meant...' David tried to extricate himself.

Kyle admonished him, laughing. 'When you're in a hole...'

'Stop digging,' finished Orlando, grinning.

'I'm not sure if they're going to keep it as long as that,' Tom said, joining this particular conversation for the first time. 'They're thinking maybe when it's all done up nicely, they'll put it up for sale.'

'Ah,' said Kyle, sounding a bit displeased. 'In which case we'll miss the pleasure of your company. Yours, Tom, and Mick's. A pity, now we're just getting to know you.'

Tom went on. 'Another possibility is...' I realised that he hadn't volunteered any of this to me before now. '...They might decide to turn it into a hotel.'

'In which case,' I broke in impetuously, 'Tom and me could run it.'

'I think,' said David smoothly, 'when it's the subject of the sentence, it's Tom and I.'

Tom and I (yes, David had been right) looked at each other. Another small pebble had been dropped into the pool with that heedless remark of mine.

'Just a joke,' I said, back-tracking in alarm.

'Who knows?' said Tom, then changed the subject and we talked of less consequential things. At least we thought we were doing that. We started asking one another whether we had brothers and sisters or if we were only children. It turned out that David was the only one of those. 'Bit of an additional problem, that,' he said. 'With me being gay – whether they know about that or not. No-one to hand the family silver on to – not that we have any silver, but you know what I mean. There's also the question of the family name...'

'You could always adopt someone,' Orlando chipped in. 'Give them your family name.' He giggled. 'You could adopt me.'

'I think your parents might have something to say about that,' said David. 'They might be wanting you to pass on *their* family name, you see.'

'I could always change my name back again after your parents were dead,' Orlando said coolly.

'You little devil,' said Kyle. 'Sometimes I think the young these days have no morals left at all.'

We broke off at that moment. The sailing boats had completed half their figure-of-eight and were now bearing down on us, preparing to turn onto their second loop. Kyle and David ducked through into the steering cabin to log timings and steady us again against the drift. This left Tom and me and Orlando out in the well deck, leaning against the gunwales, Tom and I on one side, Orlando facing us. The sight was wonderful. We were in the middle of the sea, the swell a lively but unthreatening metre or so, a patchwork of greens and greys and blues, fringed with occasional tassels of white spray. Beyond, and all around us, proud yachts that sported full rigs of sails heeled breathtakingly as they turned through the wind; their snowy canvas bellied and boomed as they raced close by at speed. In the near ground, leaning against the gunwale opposite me, was Orlando. His beautiful face radiant with the sun, with the joy of the scene, reflected my own happiness back to me. I looked at his eyes. Unwisely. They were powered up with the same luminous blue that energised the sea. I was filled with a feeling so intense and beautiful that it frightened me. I turned to Tom. Looked into his coal-blue eyes too. Just as Orlando's had done, at this moment they radiated the kaleidoscopic blues of the surrounding sea. Unlike Orlando's they were focused not on the wonderful scene around us all, but on me. On only me. I threw myself around him and, too late to care what Orlando might think of me, let loose on Tom's warm bare neck a silent flood of tears.

'There's nothing wrong with noticing he's beautiful,' Tom tried to reassure me, later that night, stroking me in our double bed. 'Orlando or any child. Children are beautiful things, beautiful people. That's just a fact.'

'I don't find your brother or sister particularly beautiful,' I told him. They'd been cross with us earlier, the two of them, for going off in a boat without taking them. 'I don't fancy your brother remotely, and at least, unlike Orlando, he's reached the age of fourteen.'

'Do you fancy Orlando, then?' Tom asked. A little sharply, so that a tremor ran through his arms and into me.

'It depends what you mean by fancy, I suppose,' I said uncertainly.

'It means wanting to have sex with somebody. Sex of any kind. Would you like to have sex with Orlando?'

'Well, no,' I said, taken aback by Tom's direct approach. 'No way. But I did find him beautiful today. Extremely so at that moment when...'

'I felt the same when you turned to me,' Tom said. 'With the sea behind you, and the light in your blue, blue eyes. I'm not surprised you felt something powerful towards Orlando, but that's as far as it goes. The difference is that you and I are lovers. You and Orlando aren't.'

'I suppose you're right,' I said. I began to feel relieved.

'You know,' said Tom, 'I find the cats at home very beautiful. At some moments extremely so. I certainly don't fancy them.'

I giggled. 'Actually,' I confessed, 'there are moments when I think the Queen looks beautiful, even now. But I certainly don't fancy her.'

'Be like fancying your grandmother,' Tom said. 'So don't worry about seeing beauty for a moment or two in a child's eyes. There's various signs mark someone out as a child-abuser. That's not one of them.'

'Thank you for saying that,' I said. I really was relieved. 'On the other hand,' I went on, perhaps incautiously, 'are we allowed to talk about people we do fancy? I mean people we might want to have sex with. In theory at least.'

'We've done it before,' Tom said. 'Why not?'

'Not about people we both know,' I said.

'I see,' said Tom. 'You mean David and Kyle.'

'Yes,' I said.

'Well, OK, then,' said Tom. 'And I'll go first. I like David a lot, and I think he looks really nice, but as to actually fancying either of them – well, although he's five years older than David, over thirty, I'd plump for Kyle.'

'My thoughts exactly,' I said. I was somehow surprised, I don't know why.

I was more surprised by the next thing Tom said. 'And would you prefer to fuck him, or to go on the receiving end?'

I had to think for a moment. To run both scenarios past my inward eye and past the nerve endings around my posterior and groin. Having done that carefully and compared the two I answered. 'Both, actually.'

'Similarly,' said Tom, without any pause for thought at all. Again that surprised me. He'd clearly had his thoughts about this in advance. Then he continued, in a less assured tone of voice. 'Would you like me to fuck you? Would you like to fuck me?'

'Both those things,' I said. Had I been standing up, not been lying down already, I might have felt the need to sink into a chair. 'But I thought you didn't want to do that.'

'I thought *you* didn't,' Tom said. I had no idea at all why Tom should have thought that. I wasn't going to ask him now.

I said, 'No, I do want that.' Then another thought struck me, which knocked me off at a bit of a tangent. 'I wonder if Kyle and David are having a similar conversation about us.'

'I should think they had that conversation minutes after they'd met us for the first time,' said Tom, six months more knowing than me. 'They're older than us, we're younger than them. It's natural. As to whether they fuck each other, though,' he added, 'that I wouldn't know.'

'I would,' I said.

Tom, startled suddenly, asked, 'How?'

I reminded him about the delivery I'd taken so embarrassingly during dinner, and told him about the rubbers in the bag.

ELEVEN

Tom became wobbly again. I could see discretion and desire at war in him. I understood easily. He was reluctant to experiment with fucking me or me fucking him, for the first time at any rate, in a bed in his parents' house.

Perhaps we dozed. It didn't feel like it. We touched each other's cock – they were permanently hard this night – at intervals, till we'd worked ourselves onto a knife-edge of anticipation. Soon after three in the morning, grey light began to bleed into the dark of the short northern night. By the time we got downstairs it was just light enough not to bump into the furniture even with the lights off.

We let ourselves quietly out of the house. Tom checked he had his key in his pocket. I checked I'd got an optimistic half dozen condoms in mine. Beside the house a little track led out of the village, winding between the fields and up a low hill between seas of waving barley. The air smelt fresh and heady, as if it had been laundered overnight. As we climbed Tom took my hand. 'Dear God, I love you, Mick,' he said.

I couldn't answer him at that moment. Instead I squeezed his hand so tightly that I nearly tore it in half.

We were high enough to see the sea above the roofs of the village below. There was no sign of sunrise yet. You couldn't place the horizon at this stage. It was misty out to sea. But there were streaks of pink among the grey, like the faint pinkness of a wood pigeon's breast. *Rosy-fingered dawn* as Homer never-endingly says. Those fingers were beginning to caress the east.

My fingers were caressing Tom's dick through his trousers now that we had stopped. Tom said, 'Lie down.' I dropped onto the grass as quickly as if I'd been shot.

We fell together where the long grass at the edge of the track we'd walked on met the half-grown barley stalks. The barley was coming softly into ear, but the stalks were rough. The grass was smoother. Both were cold. Both were wet with pre-dawn dew.

Awkwardly, because we were both lying down, we undressed each other. It was something we hadn't done since those first days nearly a month ago. We got colder and colder as the process went on, and as we rolled among the green grass and barley, our nakedness in increasing contact with the dewy green, our teeth began to chatter and we shivered. Although not only from the cold.

I feared our cocks when we at last exposed them would be shrivelled and flaccid with the cold. Tucked up and in retreat like snails. Not a bit of it. Our two dicks faced proudly out and upward. Rampant like lions.

Neither Tom nor I had watched gay porn. We'd talked about this, of course. Our stories had been the same. Seen some heterosexual stuff, and not been particularly turned on. Worried a little bit about that. Only glimpsed the odd moment of gay activity, but quickly clicked that off. In case we found, terrifyingly, that we liked that better. We realised that together now.

Still, we'd picked up enough by osmosis to know two obvious things. You could do it face to face if you were young and agile, or else do it piggy-back. We then made two decisions together without voicing them or having to negotiate. We knew absolutely that, this first time at least, we'd do it face to face and that Tom would poke me first.

'Hey, here,' I said. I reached into the pocket of my jeans, which were lying by my side. (We were both stark naked now.) I handed him a rubber and watched him as he proceeded to roll it on, pretending the nonchalance of someone who'd done it many times before. I knew he hadn't. I was impressed though. He got it on first time, and without producing a bubblegum-like balloon of air.

Tom's fingers had diffidently explored my arse from time to time when we'd been wanking together or simply playing in bed. Mine had done the same to his. But only one finger at a time, and only up to the first joint. So when I felt Tom's middle finger now worming its questing way into my hole, I felt the apprehension of a child who's had his teeth probed and scraped by a dentist before, yet knows that this time it's the preliminary to having one of them drilled out.

I drew my knees up, then instinctively raised my bum into the air. It seemed to be all the signal that Tom needed. From kneeling between my legs he dropped his chest onto mine and blindly, hoping for the best, thrust his way in.

It was a shock, but only a mental one. It didn't hurt. I was glad that Tom's cock, with its recipient-friendly taper, was, exactly like mine, a run-of-the mill six inches long. I lay back comfortably and no longer apprehensive. Tom's thrusting felt nice, though of itself it wasn't going to make me come. It was wonderful, though, in a way that had little to do with the physical. It was wonderful because it was Tom.

His first time. My first time. No surprise: it didn't take Tom long. He pulled out. 'Are you OK,' he said. A bit matter-of-factly, I thought. Then he threw himself down on my chest. 'Mick,' he said. His voice broke. He started crying. With both hands he rubbed the sides of my head above my ears. 'Oh my Mick.'

I wrapped my hands around the back of his head. 'My Mick,' I said to him. 'Oh my Mick.' It seemed that for the moment at least I'd forgotten that his name was Tom.

The sun rose on our nakedness and gilded our lion loins. 'Do you want to do me now?' Tom asked, his voice awed and husky. 'I'm fine with it if you are.'

'No,' I said. Bizarrely I thought of Orlando, and tried to be as wise and philosophical as I'd come to imagine him. 'That was your moment. I'll make mine special – separately special – another time.'

'Do you want to come, then?' Tom queried gently.

I did, but I was perishing with cold. 'Yes, but when we're back in bed. Let's descend this mountain first.'

For some reason it didn't cross either of our minds to put our clothes back on. We carried them round our shoulders as we walked back down the hill. Along the sunlit track, naked and side by side at a quarter to five in the morning, our modest physiques became those of bronze Greek athletes in the stare of the rising sun.

TWELVE

On our last night in Scotland Tom's mother took me aside after dinner and we walked together out into the garden. Tobacco flowers were beginning to scent the evening, though it was still broad daylight. Without preamble, and looking not at me but ahead of her along the path, she said, 'You've made Tom very happy. He's never been a happy boy before. Now I know why. He hadn't met anyone like you. He hadn't met you, full stop. I'm not going to be indelicate or talk about things that are private and don't concern me. But may I say I hope you go on being his friend. Seeing Tom happy for the first time in his life has meant a lot to me too.'

Then she stopped walking and turned to me. 'Can I just say, in a very general way, that long-term relationships don't stay easy at every stage. They have bad moments. But those can be got through. Sometimes with a little help from friends. I'm talking about my own life here, not yours. Don't worry. But if ever you have cause to recall this conversation, just remember you can always talk to me. Always. OK now. That's all I wanted to say. Tom will be waiting for you in the hall, I imagine, anxious to get you out and down to the beach or to the pub. And agog to know what we were talking about. You can tell him if you want.' She gave me a smile and a nod. I had to stop myself running on my way back into the house, where, as predicted, Tom was waiting for me in the hall. With an anxious look on his face.

I dragged him out the front door like a whirlwind, not giving him time to speak. As soon as we were outside I said, 'It's great news. Your mum's OK about us. She knows, of course.' Then I told him, almost word for word, what his mother had said.

His response was less ecstatic than mine had been. 'One down, three to go,' he said.

'Meaning?' For a second I was cross with him.

'There's still Dad. Plus your two.'

'Your father will be fine with it,' I insisted. 'If not at first, your mum'll talk him round. As for mine, well, that's my problem.'

'I know,' he said. 'That's what I'm afraid of.'

A deep chill of dismay ran through me. 'You mean you think I won't be able to handle it if they give me grief? That I'd give you up for the sake of a quiet life? Find a girlfriend and settle down to make a family with someone I didn't entirely love? To please my parents, like people had to do generations in the past?' I stopped. 'You don't know me at all, Tom. You must think me a total little shit.'

Now I could see that Tom was upset. He turned and grabbed hold of me, hugged me like a bear. 'Darling,' he said. It came out like a sob.

I held on to him as though a sudden wind might tear us apart. 'Darling,' I said.

We continued to embrace for half a minute more, on the sea front outside the front door, in full view of the village and all the boats. Tears poured down both our faces. This seemed to be happening rather a lot.

Eventually we broke apart, smiled cautiously at each other and wiped our eyes with our knuckles. 'I didn't know love would be like this,' Tom said with a rueful smile.

'Neither did I,' I said. 'Because we've never been in love before. That's why. But on the whole it's good, isn't it?' I grinned at him. 'Darling,' I said. Just for the hell of it.

'Darling,' he said to me and grinned back.

We'd called each other darling twice now in the last few seconds. The first time in the heat of emotion, the second time just for the hell of it. I said it a third time. Quietly, as if I was practising it. 'Darling Tom.'

Probably neither of us had spoken the word aloud before this evening. Certainly never addressed anyone with it. Tom said, 'Darling Mick.'

Now that we'd called each other that we knew that as long as we remained together we always would.

Never did a fortnight pass so quickly. I guessed that heaven, if it existed, must be like that. Eternity gathered in an eye-blink. Even the bad things turned out to be good. Like the cold dew on my naked back when Tom first fucked my arse. Like the occasional moments of chill, or of misunderstanding between Tom and me. Moments that were like agony for a second or two, but were then put right with a massive hug and a dose of salt tears. And then things were ten times better than they'd ever been. Moments that taught us about the mystery of love.

Silly moments, like the fish. Remember the sailing race? When we cast lines into the sea? They were weighted with padlocks and baited with feathers. Sometimes the hooks got embedded in the pennant at the stern of the boat, if the wind took them as we cast, and it took ages to pick them out. When the race finally ended, with Orlando blowing his elf horn as each boat funnelled fast between the marker buoy and us, and either Tom or me waving the flag, we looked at our rods and dangling lines, and at the empty plastic bucket in the well of the deck. We realised then that we hadn't caught a single thing. There hadn't been one bite. Then we all looked at each other and roared with laughter, as we all realised together, even Orlando, that it didn't matter a two-penny toss.

We spent a little time most evenings with Kyle and David in the pub. We were in awe of their wisdom and experience, of the fact they were six years ahead of us along the road we'd embarked on so recently. They realised that and, I think, were touched.

We went sailing, proper sailing, with Kyle and David and Orlando, in Orlando's father's (Kyle's brother's) boat. We got very wet, though it was so exhilarating to be out there among the waves that we just about managed not to be sick. We went inland and climbed some modest hills. We continued to scrape and paint. I cooked two more meals, which went down well (hahaha). And then we packed up and went home on the train.

Returning to Becket Street I felt I'd been away two years, not just two weeks. I'd changed, and grown up, so much. I'd only been back at home an hour – Tom's father had driven me back from from Bligh House – before I found myself missing Tom. I couldn't bear to spend a claustrophobic evening with my parents and without him. I asked my father if I could borrow his car after we'd eaten and go and meet Tom in the pub.

'For heaven's sake,' Dad said. 'You've only just said goodbye to him. You've been with him day and night for two weeks. Give him a break. He probably wants a rest from your company even if you don't from his.'

'Isn't it time you caught up with your other friends?' my mother said, trying to keep the peace.

'They'll keep,' I said.

'They won't,' she came back heatedly. 'Friends have a limit to their patience. You need to be careful of that.'

'What is it that's so special about Tom, then?' Dad said.

'Look,' I said. 'I'm going to meet Tom at the Tickled Trout. If you're not lending me the car, that's fine. No problem. I'll walk.' I slammed out of the house. Before the front door shut behind me I heard Dad say to Mum reassuringly, 'He'll be back.'

Thank God for mobile phones. What people twenty years ago did without them I've no idea. It would have taken over an hour to walk to the Trout. I'd gone about a hundred yards only, I think, before I called Tom. 'Can you come and get me?' I said, sounding pathetic. 'I'm walking towards the A28.'

'I'll be there in five,' Tom said, and ended the call. He'd sounded totally unsurprised. But more than that. He sounded cock-a-hoop. Fully in command of a situation that was going the way he wanted. And I, in turn, was pleased by that.

It took him ten minutes actually, but never mind. In these situations it always does. Another ten minutes and we were sitting out on the pub lawn in the evening sun, by the river, looking at the swans (their cygnets had grown amazingly while we'd been away) and the quivering trout.

'We need our own cars,' Tom said. He was in practical mode. 'Rich kid like me would normally have one anyway. It's just I haven't felt the need till now.'

'I could do with one, that's for sure,' I said. 'But get one with whose money? I can't see myself asking my parents for the cash. Not now. Not after what happened just now.'

'Things'll calm down,' Tom said. 'But I take your point. Maybe we should start looking for a place together, like Kyle suggested. Flat in Canterbury. Or a hovel in the countryside, like him and David.'

'Theirs isn't a hovel,' I protested. We'd been to their place once. 'It's nice.'

'I was only joking. Darling...' We were learning that a lot of different meanings can be loaded onto that one word. It depends on the way you say it. 'Anyway,' Tom went on being practical, 'as far as tonight's concerned, you're staying at Bligh House. I'll lend you a change of socks and pants.'

I liked the sound of that. For some reason we hadn't got round to wearing each other's clothes yet. Just hadn't thought of it. I wondered now, why ever not? At least the Bligh House end of things was easy now. Ever since Tom's mum had talked to me two days ago. We didn't have to worry about our welcome there.

'Phone your parents,' Tom instructed me. 'Tell them you're staying at Bligh tonight and you'll be back at Becket Street after college tomorrow.' My heart sank at the thought of that encounter tomorrow afternoon, but I got my phone out and called home. My mother answered. I told her exactly what Tom had told me to, and she sounded cool with it. 'And now,' said Tom, 'let's just enjoy our pint.'

We enjoyed two, actually, but didn't stay for a third. We could have walked back to Bligh House, we often had, but we had Tom's father's car to think about. We didn't want to have to walk down here before breakfast in the morning and retrieve it from the pub car-park.

At Bligh House it looked like most of the family had gone upstairs for the night. However, we ran into Tom's mother in the kitchen. She didn't seem surprised to see me with her son. 'Have you eaten, Tom?' she asked. I said I had. At least we'd got that out of the way at Becket Street before I said I wanted to go out. 'If you need a midnight snack at all, either of you,' she said, 'there's various leftovers in the fridge.' Then she sailed out through the door. Again I was left wishing my mother was more like that.

The mention of food makes people who didn't think they were hungry suddenly feel so. Tom looked at me. 'You know what?' he said.

Five minutes later we were sitting at our old garden table together, looking out over the view. On the table in front of us was a bottle of white wine and two glasses and a couple of sandwiches made from cold roast beef, with horseradish sauce. In my jeans pocket were eight of David's condoms. I'd had the forethought to travel all day with them there, in case I got separated from the main supply which was in my suit-case. As I now *had* become parted from my suitcase, I was pleased with my forward planning. Yes, but eight? I'm one of those people who over-prepares rather, just in case.

It was still less than forty-eight hours since Tom had fucked me in the wet grass, and we hadn't repeated that. Nor had I returned the compliment yet. The previous night had been our last one in Scotland. We'd got to bed late and had to get up very early for our morning train. In bed we'd just done our usual thing.

'Oh shit,' Tom suddenly said. I wondered why. The lights were coming on in the dusk below, turning the Kent countryside into a star-pricked map. It was a beautiful moment. What had he remembered suddenly that had jarred his thoughts?

'Why, oh shit?'

'We haven't got the condoms with us,' he said. 'I was just thinking...'

I stopped him in his tracks, fishing one out of my pocket and holding it out towards him. Not all eight. I didn't want to overwhelm him with my prescience.

'Jesus, you read my mind.' We'd stopped calling each other man or mate. It was either darling, now, or nothing at all, or Tom and Mick. 'I was just thinking, though you obviously got there before me, it would be nice if, out here, you could fuck me, this time round.' I'd expected, once he began the sentence, that he'd say he wanted to fuck me again. So there was an element of surprise in what he'd said.

But I found an anxiety then. 'Supposing your mum or dad come out?'

'They won't,' Tom said patiently. 'Think about it. Mum knows about us. Either she assumes we have sex, or she assumes we don't, or she prefers not to think about it. In all three of those cases the last thing she'd do is trawl the garden after dark to try and catch us at it. In the unlikely event Dad wanted a late night stroll she'd stop him, or find some pretext to make a big noise as he stepped through the door. And the kids, they won't come out.'

'You're right,' I said. Then, 'Do we finish the wine first, or...?'

Tom chuckled softly to himself. 'You nervous or something?' he queried gently. He was right. I was nervous. 'Leave some for afterwards. We'll enjoy it all the more.' Considering his limited experience of it, Tom could be quite wise sometimes about sex.

Then, 'Come here,' he said. I stood and walked the single pace that was needed before my knee touched his. He stood too, and undid his jeans. He pulled them down a little way. I did the same with mine. Our cocks were only a little bit excited. They jutted, rather than merely hanging, but still were nowhere near standing up.

Tom took his glass of wine and lowered it till it was beneath my dick. Then he raised it, like a barman using an optic measure, until my cock was immersed in the wine inside the glass. How cold it felt! Yet what a surprise. And there was a kind of zany, weird delight. He took the glass away and raised it to his lips. 'Cheers, darling,' he said. He took a sizeable slurp, then laughed. 'Go on,' he said. 'Your turn.' So I did exactly the same with his cock and my glass of wine. I wondered, as I took my slurp, whether it would affect the taste. It did not.

A minute later we were on the grass. A minute more and we were undressed. I was scared of the rubber, and of getting it wrong, and of making a fool of myself. 'You do it for me, Tom,' I said. And patiently – no, more than patiently – lovingly – and loving every second of it – he did.

All I did was copy what Tom had done that first time. And he copied me. Raised his knees and his bottom to help me, while I inserted my middle finger into him. It went in easily and I was encouraged. A moment later I'd replaced it with my dick. Like on the first occasion, we'd brought no bottled lubricant of any kind with us. Like Tom that first time, I used my spit.

Then there I was, I who'd never fucked anyone or anything – I don't count occasional youthful experiments under the mattress at home – fucking Tom. Tom my lover, Tom my boyfriend, Tom my man.

Like the see-saws, like the swings – like the big dipper after a time, as I got into it – it was like all the bloody fairground rides rolled into one, but with value added by the involvement of my cock. I thought of something Tom hadn't done that time. I grabbed hold of his stiff dick, which was waving and bouncing about in front of me, and started to stroke him off.

Incredibly we climaxed simultaneously, trying not to make a noise. Tom spilled his milk across his tummy – it looked like a small jugful – while mine spilled even more intimately, inside him.

'Are you OK?' I asked him, after we'd both quietened down. 'I haven't hurt you at all?'

'No, I'm fine,' he said, and shook his head. It looked like an expression of wonder, not denial. I began to pull myself out of him. 'No, stay where you are a minute,' he said. The sky had darkened completely by now. 'I just want to lie here a moment longer. I'm looking up at the stars.'

THIRTEEN

We went in to Canterbury on the bus next day. It was like going in to college, except that it was summer and so there was no college, and we caught a later bus. We did what any teenagers do in their local town in summer. Mooched around. Looked at the shops. Had no intention of buying anything. We looked in estate agents' windows at pictures of flats to let. Said non-committal mmmms and ahs as we digested the prices. Neither of us dared to go inside to ask for further information. The prices were academic anyway, whether high or low. I had no money of my own and no income. As for Tom, well, he had wealthy parents; he might have money stashed away; I'd never asked. But like me he had no earned income. Neither of us had a job.

'I'm thinking I might have to get a summer job,' I said.

There was no time for Tom to reply. A voice spoke to us. To me actually. 'Mick. Hi.'

We both turned round. A mate of mine from college stood there on the pavement. Duncan. With his girlfriend Jeb. 'Haven't seen you for ages, mate,' Duncan said. 'Where you been? I text you a couple a times, but no reply.'

'I've been in Scotland,' I said. Then, 'this is Tom.'

'Hi, Tom.' Then Duncan introduced himself. I'd been too flustered to do that. He introduced Jeb too.

Tom said, to my astonishment and horror and delight, 'I'm Mick's boyfriend, by the way. There. That's saved us all a bit of time.' Then he shut his mouth – a nervous smile played around the corners of it – and just stood there waiting for the fall-out.

'Oh hey. Well, there you go,' Duncan said a bit uncertainly.

But Jeb stepped forward and hugged me and said, 'Mick, that's wonderful news! Am I allowed to spread it round?'

We went to a café, the four of us, and caught up on what we'd all been doing since the end of term. Obviously Tom and I left out the most intimate parts. But I guessed Duncan and Jeb did too. I guessed everyone did. I was in a place I'd never been before, and so guessing was all I could do. If Duncan felt uncomfortable socialising with two guys who were 'boyfriends' he managed to disguise the fact. All credit to him for that. As for Jeb, she seemed delighted with my new situation. You might say, quietly thrilled. Eventually we split, and agreed to have a drink one evening soon.

'If you get a job,' Tom continued our previous conversation smoothly as soon as we were alone together again in the street, as if the interruption hadn't occurred, 'then I wouldn't see so much of you. I wouldn't like that.'

'Neither would I,' I said.

'It's going to be bad enough when term starts, and we're apart for the college day,' Tom said. 'I want to spend all my holiday time with you.'

I wanted that too. But now we'd come back from Scotland I saw problems looming everywhere. My parents would expect me to sleep at home with them. Unless I got a flat with Tom. I couldn't get a flat unless I got a job. Then I couldn't spend my days with Tom. I couldn't move in to Bligh House permanently, unable to pay for the food I ate there. However fond of me Tom's mum was I couldn't ask her to put up with that. I said all this to Tom. He had an answer to most things, but not to that little lot.

We had a sandwich and a half pint in the City Arms in Butchery Lane. But that did nothing to cheer me up. I grew more morose as the time went on and the hour grew nearer when I would have to return to Becket Street. I didn't know what I was going to say to my parents, or how things were going to go after that. Oh all right, I'll admit it. I was fucking scared. I was ready to crap myself. I didn't tell Tom this at the time.

We got the bus back. Sat side by side. I wanted that bus ride never to come to an end. My courage was failing me, I realised, at the very time in my life I needed it most. I'd promised Tom I'd handle this bravely, but now I knew I couldn't. My stomach felt like a clenched fist. I wanted to throw up.

We reached my stop. I got up. I turned back to Tom as I stood. 'I'll text you,' I said. 'Let you know how things go.' It took me a half second to realise that Tom was getting up too.

'Come on,' he said. 'Let's get off the bus.'

I was speechless. We went down the steps together and the bus moved off, leaving us together in the road. Tom said, 'I'm not leaving you to do this on your own.' Then he looked closely into my eyes. 'Oh Jesus, baby, don't fucking cry.'

'I wasn't expecting two of you,' Mum said as she opened the door. 'But come in anyway. Dad's in the living-room.' Dad started work at crack of dawn most days. He was usually home by mid-afternoon. We all trooped in and sat.

'Nice to see you, Tom,' Dad said. He nodded to Tom but didn't get up, and he didn't smile.

Tom spoke next. I heard his voice sound high and strained, uncertain of itself. 'We've come to tell you... We've come to get Mick's things. He's coming to Bligh House. For the summer at least. To live with me. After that we'll get a flat together.' By the end of the speech his voice was firm and purposeful. He knew he'd done it. It had cost him, but he'd made it through.

My father did smile then, though a bit faintly. 'You've come to tell us, I think, that our son's gay. I don't know why he couldn't have done that himself.' He looked at me. In a querying rather than in a hostile way.

'It isn't an easy thing to do,' said Tom, answering for me again. 'I haven't told my parents yet about me.'

I spoke for the first time. It was like the words just came out of their own accord, and I listened to them with surprise. 'I don't know if I'm gay,' I heard my own voice say. 'I just know I love Tom.'

I got up and turned to leave the room. I heard Tom following me, saying, 'Let's get your things.'

There was a limit to what we could take. We had no transport except our own feet. We packed a backpack in the end. 'We can come back for the rest with the car another time,' said Tom. I agreed. But I made sure to chuck the condoms in.

Mum was in the hall when we got downstairs. 'It's going to be a bit difficult for Dad at first. What with you being the only boy. But he'll get used to the idea in time, I know.'

'What about you, though?' I asked her.

She didn't smile but she said, 'I think perhaps I've always known.' Then she put her arms around me and we kissed. She opened the door. 'It's still your home whenever you need it,' she said. She turned to Tom 'You're welcome here too. In a few days, when the dust has settled, come to supper again. The pair of you.'

'I was so scared I nearly pissed my pants,' Tom said as we walked up the street.

'Me too,' I said. As soon as we'd left the houses behind we unzipped urgently and pissed like racehorses against the hedge.

It took us an hour and three quarters to walk to Bligh House. It was a hot day and we were sweating in our clothes by the time we arrived. We didn't phone ahead. What would we say?

Tom's mother was working in the garden when we arrived. We saw her kneeling by a flower-bed some way off. 'I think I need to speak to her first alone,' Tom said. 'If you don't mind.' I hung back, standing on the lawn, my hot backpack still in place. I thought that I'd be giving a hostage to fortune if I took it off and put it on the ground. I saw Tom walk over to his mother. Saw her get up off her knees. Watched them talking – occasionally one or both of their heads would turn in my direction for a second, then they'd turn back to each other. I couldn't hear the words that were exchanged. They seemed to be talking a long time. I saw Tom give his mother a kiss. Then abruptly he turned away and walked indoors through the French windows, without giving me a look. Meanwhile his mother began to walk towards me. I wondered what on earth she was going to say.

She walked up to me unhurriedly. I just stayed rooted to the spot where I stood, pack still on back. 'Tom tells me you're joining the family,' she said when she was close. 'You're more than welcome. I'm saying that on Tom's father's behalf too,' she added, 'just in case you had any worries there.' She paused a second, almost frowned. Then she resumed. 'Tom also tells me you're worried about not being able to pay for your keep while you're here. But you earned your keep in Scotland well enough. Did a lovely job painting. You like working with Tom, I know.' Her eyes twinkled for a moment. 'As well as not working with him too, of course. Well, there's some work for both of you here, over the summer at any rate.' She looked round at the garden behind her. 'It may all look lovely but there's loads to be done out here. I thought I was going to have to pay to get someone in. Now it seems I won't have to. Well, if you agree, that is. How does that sound?'

I'd watched scenes that ended like this on TV. I said, 'It's a deal.'

Tom appeared from behind her suddenly. He had two cans of beer in his hand. 'Get this down you,' he said, holding one out to me. 'Reckon we both deserve this, don't you?' He tore at the ring-pull and opened his own beer with a clicking, hissing sound. 'And put that stupid backpack down.'

And so I became a gardener. It didn't take up too much of my time. Tom and I worked together. Seldom more than a few feet apart. I hadn't expected to be paid anything. I'd have been quite happy with just my board and lodging, but Tom's father insisted on paying me a little bit as well. Not to the point of spoiling or embarrassing me. Enough for my beer money and an occasional meal out with Tom, and a little to put by for when I needed to buy new clothes. Not that I needed to yet. I've already said that Tom and I were the same size. By pooling our two wardrobes we effectively, and at a stroke, doubled their size.

Once a week Tom and I ate at my parents' house. The first time it felt a little stiff and strained, but it got easier with each visit. While at Bligh House I volunteered to cook occasionally. I was careful about this, not wanting to usurp Tom's mum's role as provider of food. But as time passed I found I was doing it two or three times a week.

Other things, I did with Tom more than two or three times a week. There were a good number of bedrooms at Bligh House. Some had double beds in, others, like the one I shared with Tom, had singles. I'd only been installed two or three days, I think, when Tom's mum very sweetly said to us that if we wanted to change rooms we could. Or else we were welcome to move the bedroom furniture around. She realised from the uncertain looks on our faces that she hadn't been direct enough. 'I mean the beds, of course. Choose any bed or beds you want. It's up to you.'

We chose a double, and with a great effort and much puffing and panting, hauled it into Tom's room – Tom's room and mine – exchanging it for the two we'd used up till now. Once it was in place, without waiting to make it up with sheets and pillows we threw our exhausted bodies onto it and lay there in the hot afternoon.

We must have dozed. We woke up at about four o'clock. We were fully clothed. 'Can't have that,' said Tom, and proceeded to strip me bare. I did the same to him, of course. Then he fucked me, face down, on the mattress that was now the heart and focal point of our new home. In advance he wedged a towel between my middle regions and the mattress, just in case. We were starting out neat and tidily, as we meant to go on. Tom's precaution was a wise one. Everything ended up nice and clean. Except the towel, of course.

At the beginning of September Tom's parents were going to throw a party, in a marquee on the lawn. It was their wedding anniversary, and it needed to be planned meticulously in advance. We were hardly into August before Tom's father put his hand on my shoulder at the end of dinner and said he wanted a word. We moved into the sitting-room, just he and I. I wondered, with some trepidation, what this was going to be about. Perhaps I'd outstayed my welcome, I thought, or had done something that overstepped some invisible line. But he motioned me to sit down in an armchair while he settled into another one. 'About this anniversary bash,' he began. 'Hannah and I were thinking about which firm of caterers we should call in. Then this evening we realised the obvious. We've got a professional caterer, and superb cook, living in. There would be good money attached to this, not pocket money for mowing the lawns.' He smiled at me. 'Would you be interested in doing it, Mick? You don't have to say yes, but we thought we'd offer the job to you first.'

'Oh wow,' I said. I suddenly saw a vision of myself, like Mickey Mouse as The Sorcerer's Apprentice, trying to manage an army of bucket-bearing brooms. 'Just me on my own?'

'No, of course not. You could employ people to help you. Hannah could put you in touch with a few if you can't come up with your own.'

I was on a knife-edge of decision, or indecision. I was ready to jump at the chance to prove myself in this professional way. But what if I wasn't up to it? If it all went belly-up – became a catering disaster that ruined Tom's parents' big day. 'I'd love to,' I said. 'I really would. But I don't know how I'd begin. I wouldn't know about costings. What to pay staff. Employment rules...'

'Then maybe I could help you,' he said evenly. 'We could sit down with a pen and paper some evening in the next few days and rough out a few ideas. Can you use spreadsheets?'

'We had a little look at them at college,' I said uncertainly. 'I don't remember very well...'

'I'll teach you properly,' he said. 'Would you like that?'

'I bloody would,' I said. 'Oh sorry. I meant...'

'I'll take that as a yes, then,' said Tom's father. 'And don't worry about the bloody. We were talking man to man.' He stood up. 'We'll talk again in a few days,' he said. 'Now you get off down to the pub with Tom – or whatever else it is you want to do.'

FOURTEEN

'I could do a whole salmon *chaud-froid*,' I burbled excitedly to Tom in the pub. 'Beef Wellington. That carves easily when it's cold. Pasta salad with slices of smoked pigeon breast. And for something hot...' I went on in this way for some time. Tom listened appreciatively, making helpful comments and adding a few ideas of his own.

A group of four men materialised from somewhere. I recognised them vaguely when they came towards us. 'Well if it isn't our two little nancy boys who haven't learnt to drive,' one of them said. Now I knew exactly who they were.

'Why don't you just piss off,' said Tom calmly. It was quite a brave thing to say to a group of four older, bigger men. I wouldn't have done it. But Tom, older than me by six months, had said it for me. He was no stronger than I was, no better in a fight. But he saw himself as my protector, like a parent bird, and what had to be said, for my sake, had to be said.

'Oh hey, the kid's got spirit,' said the one who had spoken. 'Maybe not such a nancy after all.' He started to move away.

And that would have been that, had not the man next to him looked at me and added, 'Unlike his silent friend.'

I don't know what came over me at that point. I felt myself turn into a mountain of rage as I stood up. With both hands I shoved him in the chest. Not punched. Just shoved. He wasn't expecting it, was off balance, and he flew backwards, landing against a table at which other people sat. Their drinks were spilled, the table went over, the guy I'd pushed fell onto the collapsed table. Then everyone was on their feet and all hell broke loose.

I hadn't been in a fight since I was about six. I found myself lashing about in all directions, throwing punches – not very effectively – at everyone who came within range of my fists. Another fist connected with my chest, I fell heavily to the floor, and was out of the fight.

I had a view, momentarily, of Tom sitting in a chair, blood pouring from his nose and a look of extreme surprise on his face. Then someone yanked me to my feet and bundled me out of the front door. For a few seconds I was on my own out there in the dusk. Then the door opened again and Tom came out, under his own steam. All I could see, horror-struck, was blood.

It covered his mouth and chin, ran down his neck, and had turned his white T-shirt crimson. 'Fucking hell, mate,' I said. Mate seemed more appropriate than darling between two boys who'd just been in a fight.

One of the young barmen came out then. He held out something like a tea-towel. 'Hey, use this.'

I was too shocked to be very useful. The barman – whom we both rather liked, and who had always been friendly with us – said, 'Lay him down on his side.' Together we did that, easing Tom as gently as we could onto the sharp stony surface.

The barman dabbed at Tom's nose with the tea-towel, then inspected it. 'I don't think you've broken it, mate,' he said. 'It's just a very heavy bleed.' He turned to me. 'Are you all right?'

I explored my chest tentatively with both hands. It hurt a lot, but it wasn't agony. 'Nothing broken,' I said. 'Bit shaken up.'

'I got to go back in,' the barman said. 'You got transport home, or are you on foot?'

'Walking,' I said, 'but it's not far. Bligh House.'

'Wait till the bleeding stops before you walk him,' said the barman. 'Come back again tomorrow and have a proper drink.' That was a very diplomatic way of telling us we weren't automatically barred from the pub, I thought. Then he disappeared back inside. I was relieved that no-one else had come out.

From the ground beside me Tom complained through the folds of the tea-towel, 'We didn't finish our pints.'

A vanquished army of two, we made our slow way back up the hill to Bligh House. I managed to get Tom cleaned up in the bathroom before his mother saw him. At least the bleeding had stopped.

We ran into Tom's father as we came downstairs. 'You're back early,' he said. Then he peered at both of us. 'You look as if you've been scrapping,' he said.

'You should see the other guys,' I said.

'Good for you,' he said, and laughed.

I thought we deserved a drink after all that. Tom found a half-full bottle of wine in the kitchen and we took it out with us to our secluded place at the end of the garden.

I hadn't realised before then that fighting made you horny. But apparently it did. No sooner had we poured our glasses of wine than we were dipping each other's cock in them. With some difficulty this time, because they were both very stiff. And we'd elaborated the ritual slightly since the first time Tom had thought of doing this. Each now bent down and sucked for a moment on the other's wine-wet dick. (As Homer might have said, but did not.) It tasted exactly as one might expect it to: a mixture of wine and dick.

Then we sat side by side on the ground, our jeans pulled a little way down, with a glass in one hand, which we occasionally drank from, and a cock in the other, which we intermittently stroked.

'We won't have all this if we get a flat in Canterbury,' Tom said.

'What, not be able to stroke each other's cock?'

'No, you idiot. I mean this – the garden terrace, the view, the run of a big house...'

'We'd come here at weekends,' I said. 'Anyway,' I went on, 'it's still high summer. We won't be sitting out here in the evenings in November. Or March.' Naming those two months gave me a funny feeling. They seemed impossibly far ahead, and yet it was as though by mentioning such far-off dates I was affirming that Tom and I would still be together then. And yes, of course we would.

'Of course,' Tom said. 'You're right. But even in the winter we'd miss the countryside, wouldn't we?'

'Well, there's always the other possibility we talked about,' I said. 'Get a cottage in the country – a hovel, as somebody said. And get a car, of course,' I added, thinking it through as I went along.

'All on the proceeds of one catering event,' Tom said. I felt his finger make a circular motion around the tip of my cock-head where it peeped from my foreskin. It was now very wet.

'We'd have to do more of those,' I said. 'I mean, I would.'

Tom's finger stopped in mid-circle. 'You know, when you said *we would...* I've been thinking about that. I'd like to be involved in this catering thing you're doing for Mum and Dad. I don't mean I want to pinch half your fee from you,' he added hastily, and his finger started its circular tour again, which I was pleased about. I started doing exactly the same to him. His dick-head was also very wet. Copycat.

'It's just that I'd be interested to learn,' he went on. 'I think it's brilliant that Dad's offered to teach you some business skills. He offered to do that with me a year or two back. Like a prick I said no, I didn't want to learn all that boring crap. Do you think he'd let me eat my words?

Let me join you when you have your tutorials or whatever it is with him?'

I laughed. 'Of course he fucking would! He's your dad. Of course he would.'

Tom started then to masturbate me fiercely. I said, 'Hey, are we going to finish this here, or wait till we get to bed?'

Tom said, 'Can't we do both?'

We could, of course. And so we did.

We ached so badly in the morning from our bruises that we had to take a couple of pain-killers each. Funny. We'd hardly noticed the pain the night before. Adrenalin, I guess.

But we felt a kind of obligation to return to the pub at the earliest opportunity. Like un-horsed riders getting back into the saddle. So, unusually, because we didn't normally drink before the evening, we took a break from gardening and sauntered down to the Trout soon after mid-day. We were pleased to see the barman who had befriended us was again on duty behind the bar. Also relieved that the group of men who'd attacked us – or had we attacked them? – were nowhere to be seen. Was that one of the reasons, the less brave reason, why we'd gone down at lunchtime instead of waiting till the evening? Because they were less likely to be there? Tom and I never discussed this.

Our friendly barman greeted us with a smile. 'Thanks for your help last night,' Tom said. 'You were really great. Tea-towel's in the wash at home. We'll bring it back when it's clean.'

'You're both looking OK, anyway,' the other said.

'Not feeling it,' I said.

'You need a drink,' he said.

Tom ordered our usual pints of Spitfire. 'I'm Tom, by the way.'

'Andy.'

'Mick.' We all shook hands, like people at a conference.

Why had I not noticed before that Andy was extremely cute? About the same size and slimness as Tom and I were. A year older than us perhaps. No more than that.

The pub wasn't busy. We were the first and, for the moment, only customers. The three of us started to chat. 'I saw what happened,' Andy told us. 'I heard what those guys said. I'm not surprised you belted the second one. Good on yer, mate, I thought.'

I hadn't belted him actually. I'd given him a push and it had caught him off balance. I wasn't going to tell Andy that. 'Well, cheers for that,' I said.

'Both of you having a go at them like good'uns,' Andy went on. 'I was impressed.'

'What happened to the four blokes?' Tom asked.

'After he'd chucked you two out the boss had a go at them. Told them customers had the right to a quiet pint without being abused. Told them if it happened again they'd be barred for keeps. They drank up quickly and left – by the car-park entrance – quite soon after that.'

'And what about the boss, then,' asked Tom. 'Will he be pleased to see us back?'

As people often do as soon as you start to talk about them, the boss appeared at that point. 'Sorry about the strong-arm treatment I gave you boys last night,' he said, joining us at the bar. 'I had to separate you all, and I couldn't have thrown those four all out. So it was you two had to go I'm afraid.' He laughed. 'That's life.'

'I shouldn't have started a fight,' I said meekly. (Me, starting a fight!)

'Well. Young men. It's normal. Healthy sign. Your hormones are all in order, obviously. They shouldn't have called you things in the first place.' He turned to Andy. 'Give the lads their next one on the house.' Then he walked away.

'He's all right,' said Andy. Again I found myself looking at him and wondering why I hadn't spotted before how beautiful he was. Then his voice became quiet and diffident. 'You know what they called you both last night... I know it's none of my business...'

Tom cut him off. 'The time before, they called us fucking little poofs. Actually we're not too keen on labels, but I guess they kind of got it right.'

'Oh,' said Andy. He looked caught off guard. He probably hadn't expected Tom to declare himself – and me – quite so readily, quite so soon as that. But he recovered himself quickly and said brightly, 'Well, that's nice actually. Nice for me at any rate. There was me thinking for ages I was...' he had a go at a Welsh accent '...the only gay in the village.'

'Well, now you know you're not,' said Tom. 'And by the way, that's also nice for us.'

'The thing is,' Andy went on, now sounding diffident again, 'most people don't know that. Working here, I mean...'

'All understood,' I said. 'We won't do anything to embarrass you at work.'

'Although a night out in Canterbury might be fun some time,' Tom said, to my astonishment. 'The three of us.'

FIFTEEN

Tom asked his Dad if he'd mind him tagging along with me when I had my "evening classes" in costing a catering event, working with spreadsheets, and employing staff. Of course his dad was over the moon when Tom asked him that. Now I think about it, that was probably the result he'd wanted to achieve when he offered me the job in the first place. And so the three of us set to work, spending a little time together at the computer, and with pens and notebooks, after dinner every evening during the following days.

We took a break from our lessons the next time Andy had an evening off from the pub. We met him there and then the three of us went into Canterbury on the bus. Tom and I sat next to each other, Andy sat across the aisle from us. We all behaved ourselves impeccably and kept our hands to ourselves. It wasn't eight in the morning, after all, and no-one had a hard-on. Using my eyes only, I did check that.

Andy told us that he shared a rented cottage on a farm mid-way between Wye and Chilham. Roughly mid-way between Becket Street and Bligh House. His house-sharers were a young straight couple. Andy got on well with them, and so he'd been doubly disappointed when they'd told him just this morning that in the autumn they'd be moving out. Who would he get to replace them? He mugged a grimace across the gangway at us. You really had to like people a lot, he said, if you were going to have them sharing your house.

Tom and I looked at each other. 'We're thinking of getting a place together,' Tom said, a bit hesitantly, 'for when term starts.'

'We're not quite sure what we're looking for yet,' I added, in case Tom was unfairly raising Andy's hopes.

'We were thinking more about getting a flat in Canterbury itself.'

'We also thought about a country place,' Tom said. 'But we'd need a car if it was too remote.'

'Two minutes from the bus, my place is. Actually we're just passing the stop.' Andy pointed down a track we'd passed a hundred times without taking much notice of. Halfway towards the farm to which it led a small brick cottage stood. There was nothing fancy or even pretty about it. But there it was. Handier for the bus even than Becket Street was, and much nearer than Bligh House.

'We'd need to think about it,' I said, afraid that things were running ahead a bit too quickly. I wasn't sure yet what I wanted, let alone what Tom did. It was vital that we found ourselves in agreement, knowing we wanted the same thing when it came to such an important matter as where we'd live.

'Of course,' said Andy. He flashed a very pretty smile at both of us. 'I understand that. You're a couple. You need to get things right. But if you decided you wanted to be my house-mates... well, I couldn't be happier than that.'

That told us where Andy stood, at least, and it was very nice to hear. That there were potential problems if an attractive couple moved in with an equally attractive single, especially if they all had the same sexual tastes, was too obvious to need mentioning. There were a few minutes of silence as the three of us privately confronted that awkward fact. It was the elephant on the bus.

We were talkative again by the time we reached Canterbury and spilled off the bus. We had a drink in the pub in Butchery Lane, then went off for a Chinese in the high street. After that we went on to a club. To the only club in fact. There we ran into Duncan and Jeb. We'd promised to join them for a drink one evening, but hadn't got round to keeping our word on that. Now it was happening by default.

Duncan, who had been a bit taken aback at finding himself in the company of two gay men last time we'd met, dealt gamely with the situation he found himself in now. Three gay men, not just two. I could almost hear him wondering, as he sipped his drink thoughtfully, if there'd be four next time, and five the time after that...

'We're looking for a flat together,' Jeb was saying. 'But they're all quite big round here, and they cost.'

'Beginning to think we might have to share with another couple, Duncan said. 'For the first year at least.'

'Finding the right people to share with, though...' Jeb began.

Sometimes too many possibilities come along at once, and it's hard to sort them out. I heard myself saying, 'We're looking for a flat for when term starts...'

But I also heard Tom interrupting me. 'We may be sorted, though. Andy tells us...'

And then we all seemed to talk at once. Another possibility reared its head. That Duncan and Jeb could move into Andy's place... We all agreed in the end that we'd need to think about things and talk again. Especially as by now we'd all had quite a bit to drink.

When the evening ended Duncan and Jeb could walk to Duncan's parents' place on the edge of town. We three country-dwellers had to share a taxi back, dropping Andy off near his place on the way. I hadn't told Andy about the catering job yet. But in the taxi now I did. 'I've got to employ a couple of people to double as waiters and kitchen hands,' I said. And, quite without thinking, 'Don't know who I'm going to get.'

'You could employ me for the day,' said Andy. 'If I arranged my day off from the pub.'

'Hey,' I said. 'That'd be brilliant. Why didn't I think of that?'

'The other thing you didn't think of,' said Tom, 'and neither did I till this minute, is that you could employ me as the other one.'

Even more brilliant, I thought. The taxi was pulling up now by the track that led to Andy's cottage. By the time he got out of the taxi he was contracted to work for me. And so was Tom. I'd employed them both. For a day at least.

When we got to bed that night, Tom and I were more than ready to have sex. Practically gagging for it, in fact. Our cocks were already stiff inside our clothes as we climbed the stairs, and once inside our bedroom we couldn't wait to tear each other's trousers off. I wanted to get my cock inside Tom, he wanted to get his in me. We tussled for a while, naked on the bed. In the end I fucked him first, face down and a bit more roughly than I usually did. Then, twenty minutes later, when my muscles had had time to relax, Tom did the same to me. And that wasn't the end of it. Although neither of us came a second time we massaged each other's cock energetically for a time before slowing down, eventually just caressing and cuddling each other to sleep.

I awoke at one point in the night, and thought back to our energetic love-making just a few hours before. There was a reason why it had been so passionate, so urgent, so intense. The reason was Andy. It was the impact that just being with him had made on us both. I wondered at that moment whether my decision to have him come and work with us on the party preparations was wise. But there it was. I'd done it now.

I did better than sausages. I did a pig roast. The whole hog. Ordered it in specially from the local butcher, who lent us the massive iron spit to impale it on. I banged the spike up its backside with a mallet (there's a first time for everything) while Andy guided it through the body cavity and Tom reported on progress as it emerged from the mouth. 'Rather it than me,' said Andy. Tom said, 'I'll second that.'

There were repeated trips to the shops to amass provisions. Crabs to be dissected and gouged, special flour for focaccia bread. There were three of us, and we were all keen to learn. To learn by teaching ourselves, and teaching each other. We wanted to do as much as possible from scratch. We prepared quails' eggs in aspic, made a ballotine of chicken, and concocted a chilled ham and pea soup in dinky little glasses with cheese straws to dip.

We had two big sea trout sent down from Scotland – I got Kyle and David in on the case – and the promised smoked wood-pigeon breast, from a smokery down on the Romney Marsh. We bought charcuterie of every description. King prawns and langoustines. A barrel of oysters, which Andy, who had some experience, and nerves of steel – in this matter at any rate – would open at the last minute. The deep freeze bulged with crushed ice.

Andy also proved to be a whizz at puddings. Chocolate mousse, French apple tart, late raspberries to be served with Devon cream, a peanut-butter cheesecake, a blackberry syllabub. A cornucopia of cheeses, which arrived from Borough Market by special delivery after I'd ordered them on the internet.

Tom's father saw to the purchase of the wines himself.

It took us three days to prepare all this. Andy worked with Tom and me part-time, between his shifts at the Tickled Trout.

For the day itself the three of us wore white. We had spent some time discussing this. We discovered that, although none of us had been particularly good at school cricket, we'd all – for some reason – held on to our cricketing whites. At catering school there were some rather fetching bibbed aprons, with blue and white vertical stripes. The college was closed for the summer, but I managed to track down the caretaker and he let me borrow three of them, on the strict understanding we'd bring them back. We each pinned a crimson rose-bud to our open-necked white shirts. I have to say that Tom and Andy both looked stunning, especially as Tom's and Andy's bottoms filled their trousers more fully than they'd probably done when they were at school. They were kind enough (both of them separately) to say the same about me.

Tom and I got up early. Tom fetched Andy from his cottage even before breakfast, while I got the oven going for the baking of the bread. And then we worked, and worked. The fire had to be lit for the pig roast early, so that the embers would be fiercely hot, but not flaring too much. Then, following the very precise order of timings I'd worked out on the computer, we fetched and cooked and carried, ensuring as far as possible that cold food stayed that way, and that hot food remained hot.

The marquee had been put up the night before. Guests began to trickle into it a little after midday. And there Jeb and Duncan were, in the black and white of sommeliers, dispensing drinks. I'd phoned them a couple of days earlier, when I realised I'd need more help, and luckily they were free to help out.

We didn't stop. There was no time even to ask ourselves if everything was running smoothly. It just ran, and we were on adrenalin, and that was that. Night had already fallen by the time the last guests left.

The dishwasher was doing its thing again – it must have wondered what had hit it, it had been on the go all day, just like us – when we finally collapsed into armchairs and sofas in the sitting-room and Tom's father poured us all a drink.

'Did it go OK?' I dared to ask.

'OK?' he said, and laughed. 'It worked like magic. Like a dream. You're a star, Mick.' Then, diplomatically, 'All of you are.' He turned to Tom and said more softly, 'Even my son.'

Duncan and Jeb left after that. They had a car, and were pretty flaked out. That left Andy, who would have to be driven home by somebody. Tom's father topped his glass up, and he topped up mine and Tom's. 'We've got plenty of spare bedrooms,' he said to Andy. 'If you don't fancy the trek home. You're more than welcome to stay the night.'

Somehow I knew that Andy was going to say yes to that. And of course he did. The three of us then stayed talking, unwinding over our drinks. We'd taken our aprons off, but were still dressed, all three of us, in white. We still had our rose-buds pinned to our shirts.

I couldn't help noticing that Andy's legs looked just as good in his cricket trousers as Tom's did. And then I found myself wondering if they'd look as good in shorts as Tom's did.

We talked about what we wanted to do with our lives. I was more certain after tonight than I'd ever been that I wanted to work in, and then run, a Michelin-starred restaurant. Andy said he didn't really know what he wanted to do. He'd wanted to be an actor a few years before, but then found he lacked the confidence. He'd always appeared a pretty confident person in my eyes. But that little admission of his somehow endeared him more to me, made him even more appealing.

Tom told Andy, a bit bashfully, that when he'd qualified in interior design he'd like to specialise in hotel interiors. He'd already told me this. I thought I knew where he might be going with the idea, but hadn't had the confidence myself to ask him outright. It's never a good idea to get your hopes up too much.

When bedtime came it came suddenly, as a wave of tiredness hit all three of us at the same time. The adrenalin had run out. Tom showed Andy to his bedroom for the night, and found him an unused toothbrush, still in its packet. Then we said goodnight.

A minute later, as Tom and I, now in our own bedroom, were getting undressed, I realised we hadn't brought glasses of water up with us as we usually did. I volunteered to go downstairs and get some. I scuttled down the stairs in nothing except my underpants, filled two glasses from the kitchen tap and then scuttled back up. At the top of the stairs I came face to face with Andy. He was coming out of the general bathroom, on his way back to his bedroom. He too was wearing only his underpants. We stopped, mildly startled by each other, about six inches from each other's face.

'I can't thank you enough for your help today, and the last few days,' I said to him.

'It was OK,' Andy said. 'I really enjoyed it. You're a great guy to work with.'

He looked stunning, standing there, practically naked, showing me just about all of himself except his cock. And even that was on display in outline: a well-defined and now swelling ridge in his underpants. I could even tell that he was circumcised; at least, from here it looked like that.

We didn't will this, either of us. It just happened. We leaned in towards each other and gave each other a kiss on the lips. I wanted to put my arms around Andy but I couldn't. I had a glass of water in each hand. But he could put his arms round me, and he did. He held me for a few seconds, so that our naked torsos touched. And I felt the now hard and upward-pointing ridge of his penis nuzzle mine through the double layer of fabric of our underpants.

Then we broke apart, knowing that we had to do that. I said, 'Well, goodnight again.'

He said the same, then gave me a smile that seemed both wondering and a little sad. Then we hopped away from each other and back to our own rooms.

I jumped rapidly into bed with Tom. My heart was knocking. I didn't know whether to make a clean breast of what had just happened. If I didn't, then I thought it would have to remain a buried secret for the rest of my life. I decided I didn't want that. I didn't want Tom and me to have secrets from each other, even if being honest with each other might sometimes hurt. I took a breath. 'I just ran into Andy on the landing. I gave him a goodnight kiss. Hope that's all right.'

'What was he wearing?'

'Underpants,' I said. 'Same as me.'

'Pity,' Tom said. 'I'd have liked a description of his cock.'

'I didn't see it,' I said, though that was only half the truth.

'Well, I suppose a goodnight peck's all right,' Tom said more thoughtfully. 'But we'd better restrict it to that. Especially if we all end up living in the same house.' He gave a playful squeeze to my own cock, which was now also stiff.

SIXTEEN

Sometimes a dilemma disappears when one of its horns is withdrawn from the equation. That is probably the most heinous example of a mixed metaphor you'll ever come across, but so be it. Anyway, I think you'll have understood what I meant.

What happened was that Duncan and Jeb found a flat for two that they could afford. It was above a dress shop in the centre of Canterbury. You could see the top of one of the cathedral's three towers from the front window if you leaned out. Proudly they showed Tom and me around it. It was in a bit of a sorry state, but we all agreed that nothing was seriously wrong with it. There was nothing that couldn't be put right with a lick or two of paint. For two people it was cosy, though it stopped just short of being cramped. But there was no possible question of sharing it with anybody else.

This left Tom and me with three main options. We could move in with Andy and solve his house-share problem at a stroke. Or we could stay on at Bligh House – leaving Andy out on a limb, looking for a couple of strangers to share his living space with. Or we could start looking for a place for just the two of us, which would again leave Andy out on a limb, though this time giving him the added baggage of some gratuitous offence.

We decided to move in with Andy. The garden at Bligh House was quietening down as autumn approached, and except for clearing up and having bonfires there was no longer a lot to do there. On the other hand, news of my successful first stab at catering a big event, with the support of Tom and Andy, had spread. A couple who were getting married in a neighbouring village phoned me and asked me to cater their wedding. It was a less lavish affair than Tom's parents' anniversary bash, and thanks to that and to the fact that I wasn't doing it for the first time now, I coped with it easily, with Tom's help of course. Then the pub, the Tickled Trout itself, no less, asked us – with Andy this time – if we'd help out with a reception *they* had been asked to provide. Job followed job. It began to snowball, and we grew confident of being able to pay our rent.

We didn't have a lot of stuff. I got my computer gear from Becket Street and installed it in Andy's place, and my parents were cool with that. Over a period of a few days we got things sorted out, and finally moved in to Vine Cottage, as the place was called, the weekend before the start of college term. There was no sign of a vine at Vine Cottage, no sign there had ever been one. It's a bit of a mystery how houses get their names I sometimes think.

I'd been a bit worried that we, Tom and I, and Andy would be getting under each other's feet. As it turned out I needn't have been alarmed. Once term started we had quite different routines. Most days we were at college; most evenings Andy worked at the Tickled Trout. He was usually still in bed when we left in the mornings, and often we were already in bed when he came back from work at night. Our paths would cross briefly in the early evening sometimes, when we'd come back and before Andy went to work. And sometimes we'd meet again – on opposite sides of the bar – if Tom and I decided to go to the Trout for an evening drink.

And if I was also worried that my one and only late-night kiss with Andy might have sown dragons' teeth, well, it looked as if I had no need to feel anxious on that score either. The episode was not repeated. Well, not for the moment at least...

Tom and I were having dinner at Bligh House one evening in November – it was a fairly common event – when Tom's father said to us, 'I've been doing some thinking about Murches. Well, not just me.' He looked across at his wife. 'I mean Hannah and I have been talking about this. You both know that one of the possibilities open to us would be to turn it into a hotel. Well, we're leaning more and more towards that. But it does depend on you two, somewhat. You see, we're wondering if, when you've both finished college next spring, you'd like to manage it for us. I mean the two of you. Tom and Mick.'

I'd tried to tell myself not to imagine this. Schooled my imagination not to run away with such a thought. But now here it was: the realisation of my wildest and most impossible dream was being presented to me soberly as a business proposition. To Tom too. We were both being offered a job.

'I watched you carefully when you looked after our party for us. I've seen the way you've been working since. I've kept my ear to the ground. Wherever and whenever you've done a catering job in recent months I hear nothing but good reports. So I think that, young as you both are, you're up to doing this. It would stretch you both to your limits at first, of course, but that's in the nature of any worthwhile job. So Hannah and I would very much like you to take it on – but only if you both wanted it, of course. There's no earthly point in offering good jobs to people who don't really have their hearts in them. It always ends in trouble. I've been in the working world quite long enough to know that. So it's up to you two. What do you think?'

I looked at Tom. He looked at me. For quite some seconds we stared into each other's eyes, trying to read each other's answer there. It wasn't easy. But then we each gave, and saw the other other give, an infinitesimal nod.

'I'm up for it,' I heard Tom say. Then, without needing to hear me voice my own answer, he said, 'So's Mick.'

Tom's parents looked at each other. The word *triumphant* might over-describe the look they shared, but *very pleased indeed* certainly did not. 'Well, that's good,' Tom's father said, looking back at us. Then his look turned grave and he said to us, 'You realise that what I've just said to you is a sign of how seriously we take your relationship, and the long-term nature of it. I hope my trust in you – and in my own judgement – won't prove misplaced. The signs from both of you would indicate that you take it pretty seriously too.'

'We do,' we both said a bit tremulously, in chorus, feeling and sounding like very much younger kids.

'Good,' said Tom's father. 'It may not always be easy, but I hope you'll try and stick with that.'

It was the first time he had ever talked in a "heavy" way to the pair of us, and it came as a bit of a shock. It was also the first time he'd expressed himself – in our hearing at any rate – on the subject of our relationship. It made me a bit thoughtful – the discovery that he took it so seriously himself.

Tom's father had a name of course, even though I haven't until now said what it was. His name was John, though I'd never called him that. But from this moment on he became John for me. He was going to be a friend, it seemed, as his wife Hannah already was.

I went at my work at college with a renewed sense of purpose, and vastly increased confidence in myself. We were doing quite a lot of oriental cookery this term, and as we progressed, I tried out the dishes I was learning about at home at Vine Cottage, cooking for Tom. Occasionally, if all three of us happened to be in on the same evening, for Andy too.

Tom rarely cooked. At least he'd rarely done so until now. But suddenly he wanted to learn. From me. Just as he'd suddenly wanted to learn a little about business management from his father after years of not wanting to, he now became my avid disciple in the kitchen. I taught him about different styles of curry – different mixes of spices and different techniques for Thai, North and South Indian, and Sri Lankan food. Together we practised the dishes I'd been working on in the classroom. Then Tom became bold enough to do them by himself. He'd serve them to me with a timid smile on his face, awaiting my reaction, wondering if his cooking was good enough. I have to say that it usually was. He was getting rather good.

'If you can't do it, you shouldn't be running it,' somebody had once said, referring to the stockpile of experience that needs to be built up by those who manage things. Tom was preparing himself for the day when we would be running Murches as a hotel together. To be able to move confidently into the kitchen from time to time would be a major asset – to the whole enterprise as well as to himself.

It was a two-way thing, though. Tom shared with me his growing knowledge of modern décor and interior design. We learned from each other, as much as we could.

As autumn advanced we learned what everyone learns who, first, lives in a small, old cottage in deep countryside and, second, will have to, for the first time in their lives, pay their own bills. The fact was that winter was going to be very cold.

We got logs cheaply from the farmer, our landlord, in long lengths, and sawed them up, to the great benefit of the muscles of our arms. To the appearance of them too. We'd always rather envied Andy his slightly better developed arms and legs, and wondered how he'd got that way, as he didn't work out. But now we knew.

We burned the logs every evening on roaring fires. But there was little heat in the bedrooms, except what came from small, inefficient and expensive electric heaters. At least Tom and I had each other to snuggle next to when we got into our double bed. Andy had a double bed too, but he never brought back anyone to share it with him. I began to feel sorry for him. Sleeping the other side of a wall from a happy couple who indulged night after night in energetic sex – even though, out of consideration for him we tried not to be too noisy about it – must have drawn his attention unhappily to his own alone state. There was nothing I could do to alleviate that, of course. At least, that's what I thought at that time.

Tom and I both got jobs. There were two reasons for this. We needed money. Despite the training in business studies we'd received from Tom's father – sorry, I must remember to refer to him as John – we hadn't factored in the fact that we would have heating bills to pay as well as rent. Secondly, we both knew that we had to gain as much experience as possible to prepare ourselves for the challenge – running Murches Hotel together – that we knew we'd be facing in nine months' time. Tom went to work at the Falstaff Hotel in Canterbury, near the West Gate: front of house, reception desk and waiting table, three nights a week.

And I had a stroke of luck. A Michelin-starred chef called Roger Wainwright had recently sold his restaurant near Birmingham and moved down south. He took on a building on the main road, the A28, which had once been a pub but had fallen on hard times and was now boarded up. I read about this in the Kent Messenger and sent an email in. Speculative job emails work only when they arrive on the day when their recipient is in a panic because there's no-one else. It was my lucky day. Roger and his wife took me on as a spud-peeler and pot-washer, two evenings a week.

With a Michelin-starred chef you learn by watching. At least I did. I screwed my head around hour after hour, to watch what Roger was doing as I did the washing up. I saw him do the sauces and gravies, make the puddings, employ the filleting techniques and astound with the presentation skills we'd learned at college but which Roger transformed with a hundred times more kilowatts of flair and energy and – let's face it, talent.

At home our schedules were shaken up. It was difficult to predict from day to day who would be in from evening to evening and who would be out.

One dark afternoon in mid-November I came home from college, a free evening ahead of me – Tom was working at the Falstaff that evening – and ready to flop. To my surprise Andy was at home. 'Evening off,' he said.

'Ditto,' I said.

'Tom?'

'Working till late tonight,' I said.

'I'm volunteering to cook something, if you'd like that,' Andy said then. 'If you're up for that.' People who cook for a living are, despite their friends' apprehensions, disproportionately delighted if anyone offers to prepare them something even as simple as cheese on toast.

'Like it?' I said. 'You just made my day.'

We already knew Andy could cook. He'd worked in catering all his life. He'd done a great job in the kitchen preparing for Tom's parents' anniversary do, and had worked with us on lots of events since then. He'd cooked for the three of us a few times since we'd been together at Vine Cottage. But, cooking just for himself and me that night, he excelled himself.

To this day I don't know if he'd realised there would be just the two of us. He'd got prawns, which he put in the oven, Spanish style, with olive oil, a lot of garlic and hot chillies. We ate them with great enjoyment. Of course we were enjoying each other's intimate company as much as the dish.

Then Andy served us a breast of duck on a bed of lentils, with a side salad and crusty bread. We finished with a dish of Cornish cream and figs. 'That'll get us up early in the morning,' I said.

'Who cares?' Andy said.

We dallied with the tempting idea of leaving the washing-up till the next morning, but in the end steeled ourselves and did it there and then. We'd washed up side by side a hundred times before. At Bligh House, at the Tickled Trout, and at Vine Cottage of course. But always with Tom, I'm pretty sure. We hadn't been in quite this situation before, knocking elbows as we washed up in a kitchen, just the two of us alone.

'You up for a glass of wine?' I asked Andy as we hung the tea-towel up to dry. I knew he would be. What else was he possibly going to say? We decanted ourselves into the living-room and I uncorked a bottle of red.

There was a sofa in the room, and two armchairs. When the three of us were in there together – which was not that often actually – one would sit on the sofa and the others in the separate chairs. We rotated this. There wasn't a particular chair or place on the sofa that belonged to any of us specially. That was part of the magic that surrounded the way things worked.

This night Andy plonked himself down on the sofa. He could have sat in the middle of it. He didn't. He sat right up at one end. He left it very clear that there was room to sit on it beside him if that was what I wanted. I did. Glass of wine in hand I went and sat next to him.

SEVENTEEN

My mind went back immediately to the first time I'd sat next to Tom on the bus. Just like back then with Tom, I could feel the length of Andy's thigh pressed against mine from knee to hip. Even through the fabric of our two pairs of jeans Andy's thigh felt wonderfully hot. 'Cheers,' I said.

'Cheers,' said Andy. We clinked glasses.

And then we sat for some time, exactly where we were, not speaking, though taking occasional cautious sips of wine and wondering what, if anything, would happen next.

'You're nice,' said Andy. 'In fact you both are. You and Tom. I kind of love you both.'

'I kind of love you both,' I said. 'I think.' Even with that qualifying *I think,* mine was a riskier avowal than Andy's. If things went wrong Andy stood to lose his flatmates. If they went wrong for me I stood to lose everything in my life. In standing to lose Tom I stood to lose myself.

Rather meditatively Andy placed his forefinger on my leg, a few inches above the knee, and rubbed it an inch or so up and down on my jeans. It was like an electric shock.

Experimentally I copied his gesture, did exactly the same to him. It had the same effect on him as it had done on me. I know this, because I heard his sudden little intake of breath. For some time we continued doing this, just rubbing a finger up and down each other's leg, our forearms crossed a bit awkwardly as if in a sort of stiff plait.

Andy's middle finger joined his index in its stroke, and he began to move them in little circles, like a French polisher, very slowly around the top of my leg, though never straying more than six inches above the knee. And guess what? I did the same to him.

The flat of his hand, and of mine, came next. Moving a little further up and down each other's thigh each time, as if we were ironing each other's jeans. By now I could see Andy's trapped boner pointing down his inside leg seam. Pointing a longer way down than mine could ever do, actually. It was an observation that made my own cock twitch in my pants. It had been hard, you won't be surprised to learn, for quite a little time.

'Can I feel you for a second?' Andy asked me, in a very neutral, innocent sounding tone. 'Only through your trousers, I mean.'

I said, 'Help yourself.' I wasn't going to make a big deal of this, or spoil his fun. It wasn't as if we were going to masturbate each other or anything.

The touch of Andy's hand came like a lightning flash. Even through denim. For a moment I thought I was going to come like a lightning flash too.

I didn't ask permission. I didn't think I needed to by this stage. I ran the flat of my hand slowly up Andy's hot leg till my fingers made contact with the ridge. It was the size and shape, and almost the feel, of the kind of paint-roller you do the corners of the room with. But hot. Hotter even than his leg.

For a moment we just palmed each other's dick through cloth, without moving our hands. Then I heard Andy's voice, less than a whisper, small as the ticking of a watch, say, 'Would you let me see it? Just for a second.'

I didn't speak. I just stood up, and so did he. Facing each other, wordlessly, we undid each other's belt and zip, then dropped our jeans and underpants halfway to our knees. The T-shirts we were wearing were short ones; we didn't need to lift their hems to give each other a better view.

There came to my nostrils a wonderful warm musky scent that was the essence of Andy. Dangerous and sweet. I wanted it, just then, to be my favourite smell. His cock, as I'd already guessed, was circumcised, unlike mine. I estimated it at seven inches; that made it an inch longer than Tom's or mine. It was standing very upright against its background patch of pubic hair. Which, like mine, was light brown.

'God, you've got a beautiful cock,' I heard Andy's voice whisper in wonder. I was surprised slightly, because the first thing he'd have noticed was that mine was smaller than his, and I wouldn't have expected him in the circumstances to be particularly impressed.

But I said what I suppose everyone always says. 'So have you.' And I meant that honestly.

We didn't touch each other's penis then. Instead we stood forward and embraced, T-shirt against T-shirt, belly against belly, prick mashing against prick. I could feel the wetness of his pre-come on my tummy. He could feel mine on his. We kissed.

Not like the last time, with chaste closed lips. We opened those floodgates of sensuous sensation and let our tongues do their worst.

And then we stopped. Simultaneously withdrew tongues from mouths. Then pulled our chests a little way apart. Our dicks relinquished their grip on each other and, though still standing smartly to attention, stood that way on their own. For a moment longer our hands held each other just above the waist. I could feel them stiffen over a couple of seconds, and then we both let then fall to our sides.

'We shouldn't be doing this,' I said awkwardly.

'You're right. We shouldn't,' said Andy, sounding just as bad.

We pulled up our underpants, pushed our wet dicks back inside them like jack-in-boxes on strong springs, then did up our jeans.

Andy sat down on the sofa again. Prudently I took my wine glass with me over to one of the armchairs. 'What time's Tom back?' Andy asked, as if it were the most casual question in the world.

I looked at my watch. 'Any minute now,' I said.

'Perhaps I'd better open the window a second,' Andy suggested wisely. Two sets of aroused privates, on parade in a small room, had presumably fugged up the atmosphere sufficiently to draw Tom's attention to the smell of us were he to come in now. Andy dealt with the window and I put two logs on the fire. For good measure I opened the door and let the fresh air blow through. A minute afterwards we thought it safe to close both window and door. A minute after that Tom walked in.

'Oh hi,' he greeted us. 'Both of you.' He looked pleased as well as slightly surprised for a second to find the two of us together. But then a slightly puzzled look appeared on his face. He said, 'It's awfully quiet in here.'

Needless to say, I was very passionate and ready when Tom and I made love in bed that night. He might have wondered why, except that we were always passionate and ready for each other, so any difference would hardly have been noticed.

What Tom did notice was the grunts and gasps that came to us through the wall from Andy's room. 'What's he doing?' Tom asked me.

'Well, obviously, he's...'

'Yes, I know that,' Tom said. 'But why's he making such a noise about it? I've never heard him like that before.'

Just as Tom and I were careful not to be noisy with our love-making, out of consideration for Andy, so, presumably, was Andy careful not to alert his neighbours when doing what just about every single male does in bed at night.

'Don't know,' I lied. (First lie I'd ever told Tom, that.) Of course I knew the reason for Andy's urgent enthusiasm in pleasuring himself this night. But I could hardly tell Tom that.

Telling Tom. Sounds like the title of a book. And it was not a bad parallel in fact. For how much detail and complexity of emotion and thought lay beneath the surface of that innocuous two-word title! There was page after page to be turned and thought about.

It had been difficult enough to confess to Tom that I'd kissed Andy that night three months ago at Bligh House. There was no way I could 'fess up to this. What could I say in my defence? *Neither of us came.* Hmm. Or, *we didn't even masturbate.*

So Tom would ask, then what did you do? *We unzipped each other's jeans and inspected each other's cock. All we did was hold each other tightly, pressing our erections against each other's tummies while we snogged. We stopped after a minute though. Out of respect for you, Tom, in Andy's case, and in my case, out of love. We knew what we might have gone on to do would have been wrong.*

Had Tom presented such a shabby tale to me... Well, I knew how well I'd have taken it. Taken it well? I think not.

Tom sensed that something was wrong, of course. Over the next few days he kept asking if everything was all right. He did this in such a gentle, tender, loving way that he nearly broke my heart.

And if I felt awkward about Tom, the same went for Andy too. We first met, after our shared moment of sexy silliness, in the kitchen the next morning. We said good morning in a friendly way, but without smiling. Our hearts were too heavy for that. We were both thinking – oh yes, I knew Andy's mind just then as surely as I knew my own – that we'd ridiculously risked our friendship, and Andy's friendship with Tom, as well as my all and everything, by doing nothing more than what ten-year-old boys all do and think nothing of. *I'll show you mine if you show me yours.* We'd courted the greatest of all dangers in doing something that was pathetic and absurd.

When our paths crossed at Vine Cottage, I'd see Andy giving me a look like an unhappy dog's. We spoke lightly of unimportant stuff. Each knew the other's heart was full of deep and difficult things. Then when we turned away from each other after exchanging a good morning or suchlike, I'd feel Andy's sad, lost gaze boring a hole into the back of my head as I went out of the door or made my way upstairs.

John and Hannah had a new surprise for us. Like the previous one it came over dinner at Bligh House. 'Reckon you two can get time off over the New Year without finding yourselves jobless as a result?' John asked his son and me. We said we didn't know but would try to find out.

'Because we're planning to go up to Murches for Hogmanay. We'd like to have the two of you along if you can make it. It'd be partly a business trip, though. Sorting out your hotel.'

Our hotel. The thought was a bit overwhelming. But a few months ago the idea of catering a party in a marquee on the front lawn had taken my breath away. You get used to the idea of big things step by step. Perhaps that's the meaning of the word career.

Tom sweet-talked the management of The Falstaff into letting him have a week off over the New Year. The trade-off was the sacrifice of his Christmas Eve and Christmas morning and Boxing Day. I broached the subject with the Wainwrights and the same deal was made with me.

The days passed and the after-tremors of my moment with Andy began to subside. I began to feel I could live with myself again. And live with Andy. And live with Tom. Which was just as well. Since those were the three people I lived with. At Vine Cottage. And in my heart too.

December the sixteenth was Tom's twentieth birthday. You're not expected to remember. Tom told me that back in chapter two. Twenty ought to be a big one. It's got a nought in it after all. But oddly enough it isn't. You've had the eighteenth one, can vote in elections, drink in pubs, and can have sex with boys your own age. And there's still a vestigial significance attached to your twenty-first: the one-time 'key in the door'. So twenty comes as a bit of a damp squib in between. Added to which, Tom's birthday was too close to Christmas for comfort anyway.

We were unsure what we'd do. Dinner in Canterbury with Andy perhaps? Or at the Tickled Trout – which for Andy would be a bit of a busman's holiday. John and Hannah took the matter out of our hands in the end. They gave Tom a dinner at Bligh House. My parents came. Andy, obviously. Duncan and Jeb, plus a few other college friends. Nobody had to cook. John ordered in a massive, up-market takeaway.

When the party broke up eventually, there remained the five of us. John and Hannah, whose house it was, and Tom and me – and Andy. The three of us had given no thought as to how we'd do the two-mile journey back to Vine Cottage. So it was agreed that we'd all stay.

Tom and I had not yet told Andy that we'd be away over the New Year. It wasn't a big deal, but still, because the three of us were very close now (no jokes, please) we felt a certain amount of discomfort about the thought of telling him we were abandoning him for a week and going off on our own. Why should we have? Murches was, after all, to be our own hotel. It wasn't anything to do with Andy. Andy wasn't John's common-law son-in-law. Yet we did feel awkward about it. Such sensitive guys we were.

I broke the news to Andy in the kitchen as we loaded the dishwasher with the last tray of used glasses. 'I'm feeling a bit bad about having to tell you this,' I began. 'But Tom and I are leaving you in the lurch over New Year. Just for a week. But we're going up to Scotland again. Have some fun. And sort out this hotel.'

'Doesn't matter,' Andy said. 'I'll be working all hours at the Trout. And my parents will want to see something of me, I expect.' He stopped then and looked me steadily, beautifully, in the eye. 'But thank you for telling me so ... considerately. You know ... that really means a lot.'

I don't know how we got there but we were immediately in each other's arms, our hands running feverishly over each other's back. Both of us were starting to cry. 'Oh fucking shit, mate,' I whispered heavily against his shoulder, while my whole body shook.

'Shit, shit, shit. Oh fuck it,' came Andy's whispered, garbled, emotional reply.

We broke apart as quickly as we'd come together. I wiped the wetness from my eye.

'I have to say goodnight now,' I said to Andy. I did have to. I was really scared now about what was happening. Calling to Tom through the open door of the sitting-room as I staggered past, I said, 'Off upstairs now. A bit pissed, I think, and need my bed. Join me in it soon.'

I'd no sooner got upstairs than I realised I'd brought no water up for Tom and me. Down again I went. The kitchen light was out. Andy had vacated it. But light spilled from the half open door of the sitting room. I glanced in, of course. There stood Tom and Andy, in a close but chaste embrace. No cocks were out, and they were both fully clothed. Andy was being given the bad news about New Year a second time.

EIGHTEEN

In a way I was relieved. I wasn't the only person who'd succumbed to Andy's beauty and charm. Tom was as fallible and human as I was. I was also relieved because, if it came to it, if Tom were ever to challenge me over things that had happened between Andy and me, I'd be able to retort, *Well, you did it too!*

Those were only minor sources of relief, though. There was much to disturb me. What I'd seen was innocent enough. Tom was, admittedly, brushing Andy's lips with a friendly kiss at the moment I'd seen them. It was like the first kiss I'd had with Andy, though they were both fully clothed, whereas Andy and I had been in underwear.

But I'd seen only the moment I'd seen. What might I not have seen? They might have been groping each other, snogging, a second or two before my glance through the doorway accidentally caught them like a camera snap. It might have been the first time they'd ever shared an elementary kiss. It might not have been. They might be... They might have been covering their tracks with great diligence and panache. Andy had wanted to be an actor, after all. Perhaps he was better at it than I'd realised. Perhaps Tom was, too. They might be having an affair.

'Anything wrong?' Tom asked when he climbed into bed with me minutes later.

'Nothing at all,' I said bravely. I could be an actor too. 'It was a lovely birthday evening. Enjoy being twenty, big boy.'

'Small confession to make,' Tom said. 'I told Andy about being away at the New Year. Almost by accident I gave him a goodnight kiss. Like you did, back in the summer, I suppose.'

'Funny you should say that,' I said, 'I gave him the same news. I kissed him too.'

'Well, that's all right then,' Tom said, more brightly. I could feel his relief run through his body like a wave. Tom, bless his heart, was no actor at all. As for me, though a new stream of different emotions was coursing through me then, I felt that, unlike Tom, I was a total shit. Miserably I began to stroke his strong dick.

Christmas was upon us like a whirlwind after that. All three of us worked for establishments, one pub, one restaurant, one hotel, for whom the days before Christmas were among the busiest of the year. Our hours were long, but still there were presents to buy, and cards to send, and people to meet and see. I don't know how we got through but we did. Christmas Day itself became a compromise – as for adults it usually is. We all had work to do until midday. Later, I joined my family for dinner at Becket Street, Tom ate with his own family at Bligh House, and Andy went to his parents, who lived in Ashford, a few miles away. We were all back at Vine Cottage by bedtime, driven there by parents every one, and we drank one small whisky together, before exhaustion sent us all to bed. As we stood up, in readiness for our short journey up the cottage stairs, we all exchanged a look.

'It's Christmas,' said Tom unexpectedly, and gave Andy a quick hug, As soon as they'd disengaged, I hugged Andy too. Then I felt Tom's arm come round me, and the other one went around Andy. For a moment we were in a three-way embrace, during which we all kissed each other on the cheek a couple of times. Then we released each other, and went up to bed in single file, saying goodnight at the top of the stairs. It had been a good moment, I thought, a free and innocent and trusting one. Yet a part of me worried, as I lay in bed that night after Tom had gone to sleep, how things were going to develop between the three of us, how things were going to go on.

There had been no sign of the four men we'd fought with in the Tickled Trout back in the summer. They hadn't returned to the pub – Andy would have told us if they had – and we'd rather forgotten about them. But then, when Andy came back from work that Boxing Day evening, he had a tale to tell.

The four of them had come in together, already rather drunk. Andy had demurely served them their beer. There was no reason, he thought, why they should remember him. Except for his ministrations of first aid afterwards he hadn't been involved in the fight at all. But they did remember him, apparently.

'Hey,' one of them challenged him. 'Aren't you a mate of those two little arse-fuckers who were in here last time?'

'I don't know who you mean,' Andy said. He said he felt he'd been transported into the courtyard where Peter, warming his hands by a fire, denies Christ three times.

'I've seen you with them,' the other said. 'All three of you together coming down that farm track by the bus stop on the A28. Live round that way, do you?'

'Not far from there,' Andy said.

'Then you do know who I was talking about.'

'I do now,' Andy said. 'I didn't when you first started in.'

'Live with them, do you?'

'I don't see that's any business of yours.'

The older guy laughed unpleasantly. 'Then I take it that you do.'

One of his mates caught at his arm. 'Come on, Max. Let the little fairy be.'

But a third one said, 'It's Boxing Day. Perhaps he'll be up for a boxing match, just like his little friends.' Which caused the first man to guffaw.

Fortunately, they seemed to be split two and two. Two of them wanted to stay by the bar and taunt Andy, the other two, probably remembering they'd been warned that if they made any further trouble they'd be barred for good, were in favour of dragging their mates away to another part of the pub with a view to defusing things. And fortunately the view of the latter two, the more sober two in all probability, prevailed. They hauled their more argumentative mates away towards the conservatory extension of the bar – the river bank was not inviting, this dark December night. But the one called Max turned back to Andy as he moved off and said over his shoulder, 'Remember, we know where you live.'

'The thing is,' Andy told us, 'I don't know whether that was just a silly remark I can forget about, or whether it's a serious threat that we all need to take seriously.'

'You mean they might come here looking for us?' I said. 'With baseball bats or something?'

'Don't be a drama queen,' Tom chided me. But I could see he was slightly rattled too.

'They don't know exactly where we live,' Andy said. 'They only saw us on the drive.'

'Which leads to a small cottage and a big farmhouse,' I said. 'That narrows the field a bit. And they might make a reasonable guess that the three of us don't own a farm.'

'Just a big hotel in Scotland,' said Tom. It was a bit cheeky of him. He didn't own it yet. But he wanted to be positive, I realised, and cheer us all up.

However, the mention of Scotland brought us to a stop. All at once we realised that Tom and I would be setting off for Murches in three days' time, leaving Andy at isolated Vine Cottage, in remote countryside, on his own.

None of us mentioned it just then, though we all saw the thought cross one another's mind. It was written in all our eyes. Instead Tom asked Andy, 'What happened after that? Did they come to the bar again?'

'No,' said Andy. 'They just had the one. They didn't have to come back past the bar on their way to the car-park entrance. But I saw them go. The one they'd called Max did look towards me as they crossed the room. I couldn't read the look he gave.'

'So we can't tell if he was joking or not,' said Tom. 'But we could handle them. Three of us together, on our home turf.'

I wasn't quite as optimistic as Tom was, or was pretending to be. 'There's four of them. We're three. They're a bit bigger than us, all of them. Also they're the kind of guys who like fighting. We're not.' For the sake of Tom's pride, and Andy's – oh all right, also mine – I added, 'It's not a matter of being gay or not.' We still hadn't told ourselves we were.

Still we were avoiding the tricky subject of our imminent departure, and leaving Andy on his own. It was obvious that Andy didn't want to raise the issue himself. He was a year older than Tom and me, and was too proud to want to appear dependent on us for protection, or to be thought a coward.

Tom and I discussed it when we'd said goodnight to Andy and gone to bed. 'Tricky one,' Tom said. 'Shame he's working over the New Year. We could take him with us.' That woke me up a bit. Though actually, I thought, what a lovely idea. But the fact that Tom had brought the possibility up reawakened my suspicion that he and Andy were having an affair. I couldn't tackle him about it. He might question me about what had happened – or nearly happened – the evening Andy had cooked dinner for me. I contented myself with saying, 'Yeah. It would have been nice. But, well, there you go. Mind you, we must think of something. Can't leave him here on his own. He could stay with his parents in Ashford, I suppose?'

'Bit of a hike on the bus if he's working late nights,' Tom said.

I wondered if the two of them had discussed that point without me. I went to sleep a bit uneasily.

By the morning the obvious had occurred to all of us. We would have to go and explain the situation to our landlords, the people who lived on the farm.

They were a couple in late middle age. We weren't friends in any kind of way. We paid our rent, bought logs from them, occasionally discussed an issue of repair and maintenance, and said hallo if we passed them on the track. But that was as far as it went. We'd never been inside their house. But this morning the three of us trooped up to their back door.

'We've got a bit of a problem,' Tom said, taking the lead. 'And we think we'd like some advice.' Older people always like it when you say that to them. 'Some people threatened us in the pub the other night. It turns out they know we live at Vine Cottage. We wouldn't be worried normally,' he said assertively. 'There's three of us, after all. Problem is, though,' he paused for effect – perhaps he could act after all, 'After tomorrow me and Mick are off to Scotland for a week. Andy'll be here on his own.'

'I see,' said the husband. The wife stood mute at his side. 'I think you'd better come in.'

Their house, which though big, looked unkempt from the outside, turned out to be beautifully kept, and beautifully furnished within. There was well-polished oak furniture in the room we were taken into, and landscape paintings on the walls, in modern frames. The room was clean white painted, with silvered oak beams showing in the ceiling and walls.

'Seeing as it's Christmas, you'd better have a drink,' our landlord said. 'Home-made cider do you?'

It was only ten in the morning but we said yes. None of us was on duty before midday. His wife went out to fetch it. It arrived in pewter tankards. I felt we'd been transported into a book by one of the Brontës.

Cider at ten o'clock in the morning raises the social temperature like nothing else can. I discovered this fact that morning; I hadn't known before.

Within half an hour we'd learned a great deal about each other that we hadn't known before. About Murches, about our pub and restaurant part-time jobs at present, about our hopes for the future. Even Andy's half-forgotten dream of being an actor was aired.

Our hosts told us they had met at the Ashford cattle market, bidding against each other for a flock of ewes. Romantically they'd become engaged on the spot, and split the flock between them, when they returned to their respective farms. Their union had resulted in a son, just one, who was something in the world of films. I didn't catch what it was exactly that he did.

The other thing that happened in that half hour was that Andy got invited to stay the week with our landlords. They wouldn't necessarily volunteer to feed him, but he would sleep at the farmhouse every night till Tom and I got back.

Tom and I felt hugely relieved at that. Our landlord was a big man with a forceful personality. He might not still be as quick with his fists as Tom and I had been, on adrenalin, four months before, but he lived in a relatively impregnable house. Compared to Vine Cottage, that was. More importantly, Andy wouldn't have to be alone and worrying, probably unnecessarily, at night.

The farmer added another point. 'It won't be just the three of us actually. Our son will be with us for five of those nights.'

We spent the final forty-eight hours before we left for Scotland in a much more confident frame of mine. Andy reported that there had been no sightings of the 'gang of four' at the Tickled Trout. Tom and I spent the little spare time we had packing our stuff. Then, the evening before we parted – Tom and I had finished work for a week that lunchtime, and it was Andy's weekly night off – we cooked a meal together, just the three of us. We cooked, I've written. Actually, I cooked. I did an oriental starter of prawns with coconut, then a curry of chicken with butter, spices and crème fraiche. Mango chutney (OK, I didn't make that) and poppadoms which I deep-fried myself.

We had a big log fire, and put the lights out and lit candles, and told stories in the flame-studded dark. We were like a family that night. A very happy family of three men who liked each other a lot. Actually, I thought, it was more than that we liked each other. We all loved each other. It made no difference whether we called ourselves gay, or poofs or faggots, or bacon sandwiches, or paper-clips.

There were moments that lovely evening when I found myself hoping we'd end up all in bed together, the three of us. At other moments I felt the vertigo of knowing that I belonged to Tom and only wanted him. And then I was insanely jealous of the two of them. It was a feeling that, for a minute or two at a time, would eat me up. The thought that Tom and Andy might already be having a sexual relationship, that I was no part of, and that they, with consummate acting skills, were covering up.

Vine Cottage was pretty basic where amenities were concerned. There was only one bathroom, only one toilet. Even at well-appointed Bligh House there had been unexpected meetings between Andy and myself on the two nights he'd spent there. At Vine Cottage, inevitably, bathroom-door meetings between any two of us were far from unusual.

One of those happened this night. Andy was walking in as I was coming out. It was winter, so we were both in dressing-gowns – though nothing else. From me at any rate, words just tumbled out. 'I'll miss you next week,' I said baldly. No beating around the bush.

'I'll miss you too,' Andy said.

Then the next things tumbled from my mouth – to my great, if half drunk, shock. 'Are you and Tom having a thing?' I asked.

Andy started. He almost blinked. 'No, we're not.' He sounded quietly appalled. Then he said, 'If I was going to have a thing with either of you, if I really did, it would be you, Mick.'

Thought must be as quick as a lightning flash. I wouldn't have guessed there was time to think anything in the blink of an eye that was all the time that passed before we were in each other's arms, locked in a tight and wild embrace. But there was, apparently. The thought was this. *You could have said exactly the same to Tom, Andy, and how would I ever know about that?*

NINETEEN

Again we set off for Scotland, heading south over the first few miles of railway track. At midday, as we raced through Lincolnshire and the Vale of York, the flat landscape became rimed with frost. It was as if somebody had silvered it with a brush.

We talked as we travelled, but it seemed we talked of everything except Andy, while we thought of nothing else. Tom and I were still friends, and lovers, and still madly in love, but there was something uncomfortable and unsayable between us, like a ruck in the sheet that ran all the way down the middle of a double bed. The thing was called Andy, of course.

Last night Andy and I had allowed our hands to feel their way between the folds of each other's dressing-gown, until we grasped each other's cock. Andy's cock, which I'd only held in my hand once before, now felt as familiar as my own, or Tom's. I felt comfortable with it, and safe. I guessed that Andy felt the same, because after a moment of just grasping them in a stationary sort of way, we started to explore them in more detail with our fingers. I felt Andy pull my foreskin all the way towards the tip, as if to see how far it would go. I ran my own fingers around the rim of his very solid cock-head. Then we took each other firmly in our fists and began to slide them up and down. This went on for half a minute while we continued to kiss, and with our free hands stroke each other's neck.

Then I stopped it. Better late than never, I suppose. Though I don't think that is what Tom would have said. I broke away. 'No, Andy,' I said. 'We can't go on with this. I'll be in the most terrible trouble... It'd be the end for me and Tom.'

'I know,' Andy said. His face looked ashamed. 'I understand.'

I mumbled, 'More than my life's worth,' and said, 'Goodnight.' Then I turned quickly away and went to my room.

I don't know what Tom thought. Me spending an extra three minutes in the bathroom – or somewhere – then tumbling into bed with him with one of the biggest hard-ons I'd had in my life. What's more, one that already leaked. I must have smelt strongly, of myself, of Andy too. Would Tom recognise that second scent? Did he know what Andy smelt like down there? Had he been down there to find out? I wasn't going to ask.

On the face of things Tom seemed to take it philosophically. Assumed, or pretended to assume, my major hard-on was a tribute to him, and behaved accordingly. He rolled a rubber onto it, then lay on his back in the bed and, wordlessly, invited me to fuck him face to face.

This meant we would be looking directly into each other's eyes. Holding your lover's gaze when all is well between you is – in a poetic image – like looking at the sun. Trying to stare into his eyes when you've done wrong against him, or even thought seriously about it, is more like staring into the sun in real life. It hurts, it does damage, you can't keep it up.

I had an urgent task to perform upon myself. I said silently, though enunciating the words ultra-clearly in my head, *I love you, Tom. I don't love you Andy. I'm sorry, Tom.* Then I looked him in the eye, at the same moment as I entered him. The second of those two things was easy. The first was difficult, but I managed it. Just.

But when we'd finished and were lying side by side, going to sleep, I could hear Tom's breath coming more heavily than usual. It had sounded less like breathing than a long series of sighs, to which no end seemed to be in sight.

Tom's parents had driven up with the kids two days before. Tom's father met us at Kirkaldy station again. We'd taken the precaution of bringing a supply of condoms with us this time. There was no need to ask John if he'd mind stopping off on the way out of town at Boot's.

When we got to Murches I immediately volunteered to cook. Tom at once offered to help me in the kitchen. Both offers were accepted. I was glad of this. It was good to be doing something with Tom, working constructively and harmoniously together. Better than simply sitting in the sitting-room, or in the pub, talking, and yet not talking about the elephant-sized issue that bestrode our thoughts.

We did a starter of herring roe: the one in Elizabeth David's book. We laid the roes in an oven dish with butter and a drop of white wine splashed over. Sliced tomatoes, parsley and a lemon twist on top and breadcrumbs on top of that. Salt and pepper, of course. Ten minutes in a very hot oven. It was a favourite of Tom's so I was glad to be doing that.

For mains, a rack of lamb the butcher had already chined, in a herb and mustard crust. As none of us was vegetarian, this was quite uncontroversial. Uncontroversial also because neither Tom nor I had cooked it for Andy, nor had he cooked it for the two of us. Of course Andy might have cooked it for Tom when I was out one evening, or the other way round. There was no way I could know, or disprove that. That was the rotten thing. In the end it was difficult to find anything that didn't hurt. I guessed it was the same for Tom also. Again, there was no way I could ask.

I don't know why travelling should make you tired – if you're not driving, I mean – but somehow it does. Just sitting on a train or plane for hours. Especially in the winter, when it gets dark almost as soon as you've had lunch. After dinner Tom and I felt quite exhausted. There was no interest in re-discovering our traditional summer night walk along the beach. Not in the dead of winter, in the dark, with a rain-spattered wind blowing icily across the sea from the east. It was coming from the north of Norway tonight, I was reliably told by John. Reliably, because he had seen the weather forecast and we had not. Tom and I were in bed before ten o'clock.

It was a good place to be, though. With Tom it always was. Sex was good between us again that night. When things are wrong between you, then sex is a great healer of wounds. It's great as a treatment for the symptoms. Even if it can't of itself cure the underlying cause.

We caught up with Kyle and David the next day. Met them, by arrangement, in the early evening in the Stewart Arms. Tom began at once by offering to buy them both their first pint. It was a way of announcing that he'd come a long way since the summer, had grown up, was holding down a part-time job, was no longer a kid.

Kyle and David were wise enough, and gracious, to accept his offer – not trump it with their own.

Looking at Kyle and David, this handsome pair a few years older than us, a few years further along our road, I found myself envying them. It was as though they knew a secret that we were still groping for. They were sailing placidly through the choppy waters of life, and had apparently been doing so for years. While Tom and I, barely six months out of childhood's home port, were already making heavy weather of the voyage, shipping big seas, uncertain if the frail untested craft we travelled in would last out. Or whether it would founder, overwhelmed by waves, and spill us out, alone and at the mercy of the sea.

'You're coming to the New Year bash, I hope?' Tom queried

'With you two there, we wouldn't miss it for the world,' Kyle said. I thought it wonderful that he could say a thing like that. To be safe with it. It showed how secure he was with David. And he hadn't just said that as a conversational ornament or flourish. I could see that he meant it with his heart.

Later I found myself thinking how nice looking David was. I hadn't thought so back in the summer. I'd found Kyle beautiful (not to mention his nephew Orlando) but found David less attractive physically, in contrast. Not so now. His nose was rather long, and his eyes not all that big. But they shone with a wonderful warm light. You could warm yourself in front of them, I felt, like in front of a coal fire. And he had high, prominent cheek-bones, whose shadows, as he moved his head while talking, added even more character to his face. I was growing up, I decided. I was learning to find beauty otherwhere than in the most obvious of places – such as in Kyle's lovely, masculine face. It was yet another landmark along the road I was travelling with Tom, another lesson from love.

'Are you lads up for another sail, this time around?' Kyle asked.

'Sailing in this weather?' I said.

'Sounds mad, isn't it?' said Tom. We'd watched the waves that day, pounding the beach and piling up white towards the horizon: white horses the size of a two-storey house. While the wind from the east blasted us – it was like a nail gun had been turned on us – with fierce icicles of sleet.

'No,' said David. 'I wouldn't take you out in this. It's all change with the New Year, though. New Year's Day brings a calm sea and sunshine and a steady land breeze. Can't make it warm for you, though. You'd need to wrap up.'

'Morning after the party,' I said, as if giving a warning to myself.

'Best hangover cure there is,' Kyle said firmly. 'I'll take that as a yes.'

There was something very special about the company of Kyle and David, I thought. I realised when I climbed into bed with Tom later that night that since meeting them at six o'clock, I'd given no thought to how Andy might be spending his day – a subject that had preoccupied me up until then to a degree I didn't care to admit, even to myself.

It took all day to prepare for the party. There were balloons to be inflated, and strings of buntings to go up. Tom and I spent half the morning high on ladders fixing balloons, and tying bunting, in the corners of the big rooms. In the kitchen too we all rolled up our sleeves and got on with things. I found this time that other people, the rest of the family and those of their friends who were helping out, were coming to me for my opinions, suggestions and advice. In the kitchen at least, as future head chef at the Murches Hotel – if that's what we were going to call it – I was the star turn. I was excited, but humbled too, by that.

Tom was just about Scottish enough, through his great uncle whose house Murches had been, to legitimately wear a kilt. And wear one he did. I know what you're about to ask at this point, so I'll save you the trouble. No, he wore nothing underneath it. I got dressed for the party with him, and much later we undressed together for bed, so I can vouch for that. He looked stunning in it. Gorgeous, in fact.

There was dancing in the big hall that would one day be the hotel restaurant. There was a band of course, and a lone piper had been hired to make appropriate noises at intervals, and to mark the New Year's start.

Some cooks put so much effort into preparing food that it jades their appetite. They have little interest in enjoying the fruit of their labour at leisure. I'm happy to say that I don't belong to this group. I munched up and enjoyed everything edible I could lay my hands on, whether I'd made it myself or not.

Later in the evening, when everyone had drunk more than might have been good for them, Kyle and David danced together as a couple. Tom and I thought this wonderfully brave of them. But nobody seemed to notice much, or to care very much one way or the other if they did. So Tom and I followed suit. It was a bit like being in a gay club, except that only four of us were gay, as far as we knew, and everybody else was straight.

People came up and talked to us about our hotel plans. We were amazed how supportive everyone was. Some had contacts with potential clients, big ones, companies and stuff. Others had ideas on marketing, on suppliers and useful people to know. Someone knew someone highly placed at the Tourist Board, another knew about getting fishing licences for our paying guests... The moment when Tom and I would roll up our sleeves and set to with the business of running the place, a mere six months away, now seemed terrifyingly close. At least we'd have each other when the time came. We'd be each other's rock. Or would we? We loved each other, wanted to be together, but deep down, right now we didn't know how things stood.

Bedtime didn't come till several hours of the new year had passed. But it came eventually and, together, Tom and I went to bed. Secure in our affection at that moment we made love passionately and tenderly, in spite of a slight anxiety on my part that we wouldn't be able to because of the amount we'd drunk.

But then Tom said it. Not me, it was Tom.

'I wonder how Andy's getting on.'

'Hard night working at the Trout, I should think,' I said. We could have texted him, but neither of us wanted to be the first to do that. For the same reason Andy hadn't phoned or texted us. Without intending to we'd somehow imposed the shackle of a news blackout upon the three of us.

'At least he doesn't have to spend the night on his own,' Tom said. 'It's better knowing he'll be at the farm. I'm glad we got that sorted out before we left. Otherwise... Well, I wouldn't be feeling good.'

'Exactly,' I said. 'Leaving him to the tender mercies of those four...'

Tom said sleepily, 'It's not as if he's any bigger than either of us.'

'Except his cock.'

OK, it was fifty-fifty. Tom was the idiot who started the conversation. But I was the idiot who had just said that. Well, all right then, not fifty-fifty. Twenty-eighty more like. I was the bigger idiot by a multiple of four or five.

I felt Tom go rigid beside me in the bed. But he said very calmly, 'How do you know that?'

'I don't know,' I said.

'Then why did you say that?'

It couldn't go on like this. 'OK, I've sort of seen it,' I said. 'That night he stayed at Bligh House back in the summer. When I bumped into him in the bathroom, I saw it through his pants.'

'He must have had a boner on for you to clock how big it was,' Tom said reasonably. He was being very reasonable, extremely reasonable, I thought. It made it all that much worse.

'It's not a big deal,' I said.

'Then why did you bring it up? It must have been on your mind a lot, for it to crop up just like that.'

'And it must have been on your mind too,' I said, 'or you wouldn't have reacted the way you did. The whisky I'd drunk earlier then added incautiously, 'You may have seen it too, for all I know.'

'Well, I haven't,' said Tom, now sounding cross.

'How do I know that?' Oh God, I was getting ridiculous. Digging a hole and going on into it, and not knowing how to get out.

'And how do I know certain things?' said Tom, now heated. 'More than once you've spent longer than usual saying goodnight to him, then come to bed with a massive boner dripping with wet.' He paused and thought for a moment. 'Well, I suppose that's something positive. It shows you hadn't just come with him.' Another pause. 'On those occasions, at any rate.'

Now I was the angry one. 'Are you saying I've had some sort of affair with him? Because...'

Tom cut me off. 'I don't even know that. How do I know what to believe? From you.'

'Well thank you,' I came back. 'How do I know it isn't you who's been having a fling with him and covering up?'

'Oh really. So that's what's been eating you the last few days. I'd wondered what it was.'

I burst into tears at that point, and Tom had to hold me, if a bit grudgingly, till I stopped. 'Oh Tom,' I said eventually, between little residual bursts of sobs. 'I'm so sorry.'

'Sorry for what?'

'I haven't done anything with Andy. Nothing beyond a cuddle and a kiss.'

'You've never come with him?'

'Never,' I said, sure of myself at last.

'Wanked with him? Touched his cock?'

'Just touched it once,' I said. 'Just for a second. Just in fun. Nothing serious.' Well, it had felt a bit serious at the time, though it had also been great fun. Also it had happened not once but twice. But I thought I'd let the one confession stand for both.

Before Tom could say anything I pushed home with, 'I'm not going to ask you the same question...'

He exploded beside me like a firework. 'I should think bloody not!!' Then he calmed down. 'We need to go to sleep. Talk about it in the morning.'

'I love you, Tom,' I said in a voice that sounded smashed to pieces.

'I love you too,' he said. I heard him start to shake with suppressed sobs.

TWENTY

When the morning came, talk was the last thing we wanted to do. Didn't want to talk about Andy, that was sure. But more than that, we didn't want to talk about anything. Full stop.

Our silence at the breakfast table was presumably attributed by everyone else to a New Year hangover. This provided a cloak of fortune, if you like, which concealed from everyone the otherwise very obvious fact that we'd had a God-almighty row.

Mind you, the hangovers were genuine enough. Cleaning my teeth after breakfast, I felt as though someone was pulling them out with pliers. Even combing my hair, I felt the teeth of the comb like a chain-harrow across my scalp. Kyle had said that a morning's sailing would be the best possible cure for this affliction. I sincerely hoped he was right about that. I could only imagine that Tom's thoughts were the same. I couldn't ask. At any rate the planned excursion on the sea would keep the two of us occupied. It would give us other company. We would not have to spend the morning turned in on the knocked-about shambles of our relationship, or continuing to do damage to our bruised and silent selves.

And at least we were both going. We walked down towards the quay together. In near silence, but at least together. It could have been worse: we might not even have done that. Our arrival at the quayside coincided exactly with that of Kyle and David. And Orlando – who we hadn't expected. He was the only one of us who was not suffering from the after-effects of the night before.

Predictions about the weather had been right. The sun shone from a steel-blue sky. The wind was sharp still, but not as cold or as strong as the easterly that had blown in from the sea for the past few days. It had backed during the night, and now had to cross the whole of Scotland's serrated surface before reaching us, which had greatly slowed its speed. Nor was it any longer driving the sea in upon the land, piling it up in pleats that towered as they neared the shore. Instead, in the lee of the coast, the water's surface gleamed silver and pewter beneath the sky, the sun sparking back from wavelets an unthreatening foot or two in height.

Orlando's sailing skills had come on in leaps and bounds since the summer. This shouldn't have surprised us. My cooking and catering skills had done the same, so why not his? He it was who hoisted the sails, running the halyards through their automatic pulleys at the touch of an electric switch. He it was who adjusted the trim for the wind's direction and strength. Kyle, who was at first busy checking equipment, then simply ran an appraising eye over Orlando's efforts and pronounced them good. And then we pushed off from the quayside, and sailed out to sea.

It was lovely out on the water, on a surface that looked like crumpled aluminium foil. But it was cold. We'd all brought sweaters and fleeces and waterproofs with hoods attached, as well as gloves. But the wind grew fiercer as we left the lee shore behind, even though the waves did not.

We took it in turns at the helm. It has to be said that when it was my turn or Tom's turn, Kyle or David would stand a very close guard behind us or beside. After half an hour at sea, Tom at the helm and David with him, Kyle came and sat next to me, leaning against the gunwale just a few feet away. He leaned towards me and bawled close up to my ear, 'I can't help noticing you and Tom not talking much today.'

Despite the volume at which the question was delivered – the roar of the wind was the reason for this – it was the most intimate thing Kyle had ever asked me. I might have been piqued, but because it was Kyle I felt complimented by his observation instead.

I answered in the same intimate way. 'We had our first row last night,' I yelled back at him, competing with the wind.

'What about?' roared Kyle.

'What do you think?' I shouted back.

'Another guy, I guess.'

There was no question of David and Tom hearing any of this, even though they were just a foot or two away. Nor Orlando, perched like an off-centre figurehead and gazing ahead of him like Sir Walter Raleigh in the painting of him as a boy.

'The guy we're living with. Andy. He seems to have fallen a bit for both of us. And both of us have fallen for him.'

'Fallen for...?'

I clearly hadn't shrieked it loud enough. 'Fallen for Andy. Fallen for him.'

It wasn't a moment for beating about the bush, Kyle clearly thought. 'Have you all had sex together?' he boomed.

I noticed then that David was leaning very close up behind Tom and saying something in his ear. There was no point, in the circumstances, in even attempting to overhear.

'Not really,' I bawled. 'I mean, I don't know what Tom and Andy have done – if anything – and that's part of the problem – I know what Andy and I have done – obviously – but I'm not sure if you'd really call it sex.'

'Try me,' shouted Kyle.

So, at a truly operatic level of decibels, I broadcast the story of Andy and myself. Of our first meeting, growing friendship, moving in to Vine Cottage. Of our encounter outside the bathroom. Of dinner cooked for me. Of kisses. Of clothes pulled off. Of erect cocks touched and fondled. Of yet more kisses. Of gazes held between blue eyes. Kyle heard me out – he only just heard me at all. While the wind took the story of my folly, and Andy's, and ran with it, and roared with it, and spread my tale at gale-force volume across the thousands of square miles of the cold North Sea.

'And now you want to know what you should do,' Kyle hollered matter-of-factly, his mouth a half-inch from my ear. I nodded in reply.

I'd noticed that now Orlando had the helm, and David and Tom were sitting across the cockpit from us. Their heads were as close as Kyle's and mine were. Their conversation looked as animated as ours was, to judge from their faces and over-working jaws. Of course, not a word nor breath of it could we hear.

'You love Tom still?' Kyle asked me. Again I nodded back.

'And would do if you found he'd slept with Andy?'

'Of course,' I bellowed in a staunch fortissimo. I was glad of the shouting then. Without it I might have had to cry.

'Then you can be sure that Tom would answer the same way. I promise you, with all my heart, and from all I've learned about the world, that nothing's gone wrong between the two of you that can't easily be put right. Nothing's lost. By now you've as good as won. I know that. I can tell.' In full view of Tom opposite he put his big hand on my waterproof-trousered knee and grasped it like a vice.

'You need to know a few things, though.' Kyle roared on. 'Will you let me be the one who tells you them, though?'

'Of course I will. I beg you. If you can help me, help me, please. I'd want to hear it from you more than anyone, what I must do. I trust you, Kyle.' It was no more than the truth, delivered fortississimo.

'You've told me you'd still love Tom even if he'd slept with Andy. Right? Then it can't make any difference if he's slept with him or not. And because it doesn't make a difference you don't need to find out. Never question him on that subject again.

'The next thing you must do is move out of Vine Cottage, you and Tom. Andy will have to find a new tenant or two, but he'll manage it, and it's his problem anyway, not yours. You'll never get things right if the three of you go on living there.'

'He's very lonely,' I yelled.

'Then find him someone else. Put him in touch with other friends if you can. And if you can't, then don't go on worrying about it for ever. That's also his problem to sort out, not yours.' He paused, and the wind shrieked into the silence, filling it till it overflowed with noise. Kyle fought the wind away. 'Can I ask you something a bit personal?'

'Fire away,' I gasped. What could be more personal than what we'd exchanged just now?

'Have you ever, lying in bed together, Tom and you, held each other and whispered together something like the marriage vows? To have and to hold … and so on.'

'Oh yes.' We'd done exactly that once, back in the late summer, in bed together at Bligh House. The memory of it came back as if it had been yesterday.

'And did you remember all of it?'

'It was a bit approximate. We got most of it. It's the thought, the intention that counts, isn't it?'

'Forsaking all others,' I just heard Kyle say.

'I think we forgot that bit,' I croaked hoarsely now.

'It's easy to forget that bit,' Kyle croaked back at me through the wind's teeth. 'But that's the big one. Trust me on this if on nothing else. It's the hardest vow of all.'

'What did Kyle say to you, all that time?' Tom asked. We were talking, as we walked back from the quay towards Murches. The sun still shone, the day – January 1st – was still cold, but we were out of the wind.

'He told me we should move out of Vine Cottage,' I said. It was lovely to be talking quietly, sensibly, and evenly, with Tom. 'And that he – I mean Andy – needed to sort his own life out, without involving us.'

'That's more or less what David said to me,' admitted Tom.

'That was brilliant back there, wasn't it?' I said to Tom, changing the subject, though of course not changing it at all. 'A morning on the sea.'

'Too right it was,' Tom said.

We'd done it. We'd come through. Tom had told me what David had said to him. I'd told Tom what Kyle had said to me. I didn't ask what Tom had had to cough up, in confessional terms, to merit such advice. And Tom was wise enough not to ask what I'd told Kyle.

Tom turned sideways and looked at me. 'You're looking good, kid,' he said.

I said, 'Happy New Year.'

We found some leftovers in the fridge when we got in. We ate them – washed them down with lemonade. Then, though it was only mid-afternoon, but already getting dark, we went to bed … and stayed there till the next day.

'You know,' I said. 'It's funny about Orlando. Back in the summer I was worried I was getting a thing about him. Yesterday I realised he was just an ordinary twelve-year-old boy.' He'd had a birthday since we'd first met. 'He's nice. Lovely, if you like, but...' I didn't know how to put this. 'I realised yesterday that he wasn't a threat any more.'

'What do you mean?' Tom knew what I meant. He knew I knew he knew. He was just teasing me. A little gentle punishment for what had gone before.

'I mean, a threat to the way I thought of myself. I know now that I wasn't going to jump off a cliff to follow him. Wouldn't walk over broken glass if he asked me to. I wasn't going to put him in front of you.'

'I should hope not!' Tom laughed, and then I laughed too.

We both knew the conversation was only a little bit about Orlando. Orlando stood for other things, and other people, too.

We were walking up the hill behind Murches. Up the track to the place where we'd had our first fuck half a year ago. Half a year! Half a lifetime where experience and growing up were concerned.

We reached the spot, approximately, where we'd first done that. Me on my back in the prickling, scratchy barley stalks, Tom, naked, shivering on top of me. There was no barley now, of course. No long stems of waving summer-seeding grass. The ground beside the path was ploughed and double-harrowed. All was bare earth. In the crevices between the rough lumps of soil, fine shards of ice stretched across, serrated like thistle leaves, where water had drained away beneath. And everywhere the ground was spiked silver with frost.

I felt a shudder as I looked at that little bit of ground. Summer dew to winter ice in the blink of memory's eye. I felt Tom's arm steal round my shoulder then. 'That was the past,' he said. 'It's the past you're looking at.

Remember the good things, forget the bad. Let's move on to the future now.'

Tom would never have come out with that on his own. He wasn't that sophisticated or worldly-wise. That must have been something David had said to him yesterday, in the eye of the wind, on the bright North Sea. Inwardly I smiled. I reached out to grasp Tom's cold hand, but found it already on its inbound journey towards mine.

TWENTY-ONE

John and Hannah, Tom and I, were having a business meeting. We had a lot of those during that Scottish week.

'I don't think, Murches,' Tom said.

'It's an ancestral name,' said John. 'Murches it's always been.'

'It sounds old and dark. Scottish baronial. Old, very old, hat.'

John said, 'What's wrong with that?'

I thought I was going to have to say something, and risk John's wrath. But Hannah, bless her, said it first.

'The boys are going to have to run it. They're the one's we're all counting on to make the hotel pay its way. We're in the twenty-first century. Tom and Mick know it better than we do. Let them have their say.'

John sighed. But he did it good-naturedly. 'All right.' He looked at his son and then at me. 'Give me a better name and you win me over. Go ahead.' He sat back in his chair. We were gathered around the mahogany dining-room table; it was where our board meetings were now always held.

There was a silence. Neither Tom nor I had given this a thought, separately or together. We only knew, or felt, that Murches, as the name of a hotel, was a bit of a bummer from a sales and PR point of view.

I piped up suddenly, though without knowing what was going to come out. 'Tommick's,' I heard myself saying. 'With an apostrophe before the S. A big jaunty apostrophe, long and curving as a monkey's tail.'

There was a major silence after I said that. One of those knife-edge silences when you know things could go either way, and whichever way they do go will make a difference to everything that happens to the rest of your life.

'Tommick's,' said John. He rolled the two syllables around his mouth and swished them over his tongue like a wine buyer tasting an unknown claret.

'Tommick's,' his wife said, enunciating the word in a sensible, down to earth way. 'I rather like that.'

'I think it's brilliant,' said Tom suddenly. It hadn't been his idea, and I hadn't tried it out on him in advance. It had just popped out of my mouth, the way his dick did sometimes, when I wasn't concentrating and took my mind off the ongoing blow-job. But he thought my idea was brilliant. I loved him at that moment more than ever for that.

'Tommick's!' said John. 'Bloody hell. What would Uncle Hamish have ever thought?!' He laughed then. 'OK, boys. You win. It's your future, not mine, we're looking at. If it all goes wrong, then on your heads be it. If it goes well ... then I wish you all the luck in the world.'

Once more we were on the train south, plunging like a shooting-star out of the Scottish sky all down the map towards the flat floor of the south. Why is the north always at the top, and the bottom the south? Maybe you know the answer. I don't.

But that conundrum was not the one that preoccupied us as we hurtled, meteor-like, towards what was going to happen to us next. 'What are we going to do about Andy?' Tom voiced our immediate concern, speaking for us both.

'Find him a boyfriend, Kyle told me,' I answered. 'But that's easier said than done.'

'Well, step by step,' said Tom. 'The first thing is, we have to tell him we're moving out of Vine Cottage and back to Bligh House.'

My heart hurt, hearing that. I knew how I would feel if my two best friends were to come back from a weekend in Scotland and, in the middle of cold winter, tell me they were walking out.

Tom reached out his hand and took mine. We were sitting next to each other, facing two other people as we sliced through the Borders. Tom no longer cared what bystanders might think. 'I know what you're thinking,' he said. I squeezed his hand tightly. I knew now that, when it came to knowing what I was thinking, Tom always would.

'We'll manage this,' Tom said. 'When we get back to Wye this evening, why don't we go straight to the Tickled Trout? We'll see him there...' Him. He, how we handled him, how we comported ourselves in the manner we handled him, would hold the key to what happened to us for the rest of our shared life.

How that journey funnelled down, narrowed itself like a dart, as we fell weightless into Kings Cross, dived, holding our breaths, through the Underground system, emerged spluttering on the bank of the Thames, to capture our last train of that long day, out of Charing Cross.

Without thinking about where we would sleep that night, Vine Cottage or Bligh House, we dragged our baggage the two hundred yards from Wye station, across the fish-quivering Stour, and into the Tickled Trout.

Expecting to see Andy behind the bar as soon as we entered the place, we were oddly deflated to find that he wasn't there at that particular moment. But our attention was also caught – at least mine was – by the appearance of a young man sitting at the bar on one of the high stools on which Tom and I usually perched when talking to Andy on the other side of the counter.

He looked about five years older than us. His hair was a rich dark chestnut, almost chocolate, colour and when he turned to look at us it was out of deep expressive brown eyes, framed with elegant brows and cheekbones and a straight but not too long nose. I haven't given a good impression of what he looked like. More useful to say that he had film-star looks.

He gave us a nod, and we nodded back. How could we not? Then Andy appeared from behind the scenes, and the beautiful visitor turned back to him. The look they exchanged... Again, it's an impossible thing to describe. But we've all seen it. And Tom and I had lived it. It's the look people exchange when they're deeply in love.

Then Andy caught sight of us. 'Oh hey,' he said. 'Welcome back.' Then, 'This is James. James, this is Tom and Mick, who I was telling you about.'

'I worked out who they were as soon as they came in,' said James. He had a lovely rich baritone voice. 'I just didn't have time to introduce myself.'

We all introduced ourselves then, and shook hands. And then we talked. There was a hell of a lot to talk about.

We talked together, Andy across the bar from us – though he got called away at frequent intervals – until it was time for him to finish work, and then we all went back to Vine Cottage, and went on talking till the small hours.

'Did those four blokes show up?' was one of the first questions Tom and I asked.

'No,' Andy said. 'But James and I had a good time prowling round looking for them in the dark at night, armed with sticks.'

But the bigger question was, where on earth had James come from, and how had he tumbled so suddenly and spectacularly into Andy's life?

They told the story together, competing, it almost seemed, to get it out.

Andy began. 'I knew, my first night at the farm after you'd gone to Scotland, that my hosts' son would be arriving from America the next day, but I didn't give that much thought. Then, next evening while I'm here at work, this amazing guy...' Andy stretched an open-palmed hand across the counter to show who he meant '... walks into the pub.'

'I came in,' James continued, 'and saw this little vision here behind the bar. It took only a second to realise I'd seen him before. Last time I was visiting my parents, a year ago, I'd seen the same vision walking down the farm track. I was in a car, he was walking towards the bus stop. I was too shy to stop and ask him if he wanted a ride. How stupid can you get?' He laughed ruefully at this. 'I didn't connect him with Vine Cottage or ask my folk about him. I should have done. As it was I wasted a whole year of my life.'

'And of mine,' Andy said.

'We're making up for it now.' James gave Andy that special smile at this point. 'Anyway,' he went on, 'this second time I wasted no time. I introduced myself, and because of where I'd first seen him I told him I was staying with my parents and where they lived.'

'And I said,' Andy interrupted, 'that I was spending the next few nights in his parents' house.'

'I stayed in the pub till closing time,' James said. 'I don't usually do that. Then I took Andy home with me. The parents had gone to bed.'

'We tiptoed up the stairs together. Kissed on the landing...'

I knew this scenario with Andy only too well.

'And I asked him,' James continued very matter-of-factly, 'if he'd sleep with me that night.'

'The rest is history,' Andy said.

'Do your parents know?' I asked James. 'I mean, about what's been going on under their roof.'

'I think by the time I told them next evening that I was going to spend the night at Vine Cottage they'd figured it out. They've known I'm gay for a long time. Though it's not something they like to think about. Me being gay in the States seems easier for them to deal with than having a gay farm-boy son about the house.'

'So I'm moving back to the States with James,' Andy said simply, as though that were the most natural thing in the world to happen next.

'You're doing what?' Tom said.

'It's not as crazy as you might think,' James said. 'I've got a massive role coming up. I was looking for a personal assistant to handle some of the stuff.' He hadn't had to spell out the fact that he was an actor. We'd kind of figured that out.

'I know you haven't heard his name yet,' Andy put in. 'Neither had I, I must admit. But he's hot-tipped to be the next big thing over there...'

'Come on,' James reproved him gently. 'Let's not count our chickens before they come home to roost. Or something like that.' He chuckled. 'But seriously,' he went on, 'you may have noticed that Andy has a look.'

We both nodded. We certainly had.

'I think he's got a future over there. A small role here and there to start perhaps. But someone'll spot him. Those eyes of his...'

(Yes, yes, James, we had noticed those.)

'My God,' said Tom. 'It's a hell of a lot to take in all at once. When's this all going to happen?'

'In a fortnight,' said Andy. 'I've already given in my notice at the pub.'

'And your parents?' I queried. 'I mean both your sets of parents. Are they all OK about this?'

'Andy told me the story about you two confronting Mick's parents as a couple,' said James. 'We took a leaf out of your wise book. Went to see Andy's folk in Ashford and broke the news to them.'

'I think that having a boyfriend who's a film star may have made it a bit easier for me,' Andy said, a bit bashfully.

'And my parents were cool about it anyway,' said James. 'Like I said, the gay son out west with his beautiful boyfriend is easier for them to deal with than two gay farm-boy lovers on their doorstep.'

I said, 'We were planning to move out of Vine Cottage anyway.' I didn't spell out the reason we were planning to do that. Nor did either of them ask us. All that was water under the bridge now. 'Until we move up to Scotland permanently we'll be living in the comfort of Bligh House.'

The next few days were like living in a pressure-cooker that someone's taken the lid off and let the steam out of. Andy worked his final shifts at the Trout. I had my shifts at the Wainwrights' restaurant, and Tom had his at the Falstaff Hotel. But in between we met up and fooled around, and told each other the silly secrets of our hearts, knowing that we couldn't hurt one another any more.

We didn't have to go to the airport with Andy and James to see them off. But we did. All the way to Heathrow by train and tube. It took an age. There was a moment before check-in when Tom and James had gone off for a pee – OK, I trusted them on this – and left Andy with me. 'Apart from anything else,' Andy took this opportunity to tell me – and I already knew about all the anything elses – 'he's got the most amazing cock.' He made a big fish gesture with his hands. OK, I realised that was approximate. But I, who'd thought Andy's own dimensions were impressive when I'd tested them with my fingers a few months back, was prepared to believe Andy, when he took the trouble to reveal that.

The good-bye, when it came a minute later between the four of us, was a sweet sorrow ... as a writer greater than you may be, or than I certainly am, once said.

Tom and I were back in Vine Cottage that night. For almost the last time. The warmth of Bligh House beckoned us a day or two hence. We looked forward to that. But for tonight we snuggled hard against the cold, just the two of us at Vine Cottage, and we didn't want to be anywhere else.

'I'm sorry I can't offer you the life of a film star,' Tom said as we cuddled. It had been a roller-coaster day. 'Or the looks.'

'Your looks are the only ones I want,' I said. 'Film stars... Take them or leave them, I do.'

Tom responded with a laugh and a hearty grab at both my thighs.

'I love you,' I said. I said this every day now. So did he. I wanted to say a bit more tonight. The words just came to me. I'd last heard them in a North Sea gale. 'Forsaking all others,' I said.

Tom squeezed me. 'Forsaking all others,' he repeated. There was a silence for a moment as he thought about this, while absently he began to stroke my inner thigh. 'My sentiments exactly. But where did that come from? Hey, that's weird!'

TWENTY-TWO

We went back to college, Tom and I. We sat side by side on the same old bus. We parted at the bus station. We said, see you this afternoon, turned away from each other to walk to our different bits of the college... And each and every morning, that parting, which would separate us for a mere seven hours, still hurt.

Then in the afternoons, when we met again at the bus station for the journey back to Bligh House, our reunion was like the biggest thing on earth.

We returned to our part-time jobs, but we only did them at weekends now. After all, we lived at Bligh House and were charged no rent.

But we were kept busy with Tommick's. Working at a distance from the place in terms of miles, perhaps, but heavily involved, via computer and telephone, in setting everything up. Kyle and David were still working on the building themselves, and keeping an eye on the contractors that came in to do specialist jobs. Tom was busy discussing décor and furnishings with the people who were up there making a reality of his design ideas. I was writing menus, dreaming up dishes, and costing them to within a penny of their lives. We talked to Kyle and David and texted them, every day.

During the Easter break we went up there. Some things could only be sorted on the spot. Bookings had come in from corporate clients already, even though we wouldn't be open for another three months. Among the reservations we found a Mr and Mrs Smith, who'd booked for the first three nights. But no phone number accompanied the name. No email or postal address. 'Oh, who took that one?' I said to Tom. It must have been Kyle or David. We didn't take it up with them; they'd been doing so much for us and had got everything else right.

'It's probably a wind-up,' said Tom. 'Andy and James having a laugh. But we'd better keep a room free for the Smiths. Just in case.'

Although spring was still in its early stages here, the weather was sparkling and bright. We found time occasionally for walks among the hills, and at the weekend we sailed along the coast with Kyle, David and the rapidly growing Orlando, all the way to Kirkaldy and back.

Our return to southern England was a short one. Our last brief term at college, studded with final exams. We both found the exams a bit of a diversion. With our big new jobs ahead of us at Tommick's claiming the best part of our time and attention, we weren't too worried about whether we failed our exams or passed. Perhaps for that reason we were very relaxed about them, and because of that, did them well. When the results came through at the end of term we found we'd both passed with top grades. And then we went back up north.

This time we drove. We needed a car for the business, we all realised. Tom's father saw it as an investment in the enterprise, and put the money up front. Just one car between the two of us, but a big and powerful one that made easy work of the hundreds of miles between Scotland and the south. One car between the two of us. It was enough to be going on with. It was no hardship to share things with Tom. Like we shared our double bed. It was more than enough.

And then, two days before we were due to open, disaster struck. The Health and Safety Executive did their final inspection of the hotel. A routine formality, we thought. But they turned to us very seriously after we'd walked them around the place, and said the fire doors weren't right.

'What do you mean, they're not right?'

'We mean you can't open this weekend.'

'They were fitted exactly in accordance with the regulations,' I protested. 'Every detail's right.'

'According to the old regulations, yes,' the inspector said. 'But the regulations were modified in March.'

'How were we to know that?' Tom objected. 'You should have said.'

'We did,' said the unsmiling man in front of us. 'We sent a letter.' He opened his briefcase and took out a copy of it. It was clearly worded, and clearly addressed to us. It must have got overlooked.

'What can we do, then, if we want to open on time?' I asked.

The inspector sighed. 'Well, you could get them altered easily enough, but it would take time. We'd have to schedule a re-inspection for Saturday morning.' That was just thirty-six hours away. The man looked at the four of us. Tom and me. Kyle and David. 'I suppose you might just about manage it. If you all worked through the nights.'

And so that is what we did. It's what you have to do if you're your own boss. Tom and I had little experience of carpentry. Well, that was true as of that Thursday afternoon. By Saturday morning we had lots.

We were on tenterhooks when inspection time arrived. The first guests were checking in that afternoon. The stores were full of expensive food ready for the weekend. If we didn't open, meat, fish, vegetables, cheese and so on would all go to waste. Our guests would take their custom elsewhere and their tale of disappointment with them. Recovery would be difficult.

We all walked round the building. 'Well, this one's OK,' the inspector said, when he'd examined the first fire door we came to. Our spirits dared to rise a bit. 'And this one too,' he said when he'd looked at the next. When he'd checked the final door and pronounced it satisfactory our spirits soared. Our dour inspector turned to us. 'You've done a grand job, lads,' he said. 'You're OK to open. I didn't think you'd get there in the time, though. I take my hat off.' And to our amazement he smiled at us.

We didn't open with a party, or a preview, or any kind of fanfare. We just opened the doors, and the young lady we'd employed as a receptionist walked behind the desk. I'd meant to be ready to greet the first guests personally, but, called away to deal with some minor detail, I arrived a few seconds too late. But I heard them as I walked around the corner. Heard them before I saw them. 'Mr and Mrs Smith,' the man was saying. And the woman added, 'We booked back in March.'

I knew those voices as well as I knew my own. They belonged to my father and mother. I felt a lump in my throat. I didn't know how much they meant to me until that moment. I ran up to the desk and took my mother in my arms.

That evening I cooked. And cooked. Name any dish you want to and I'll bet you I chased it around a skillet or frying pan, or put it in the oven, or flashed it under the grill that night. At least, that's how it felt.

The waiters worked their socks off, the washers-up washed up. A young friend of David's served behind the bar. It was hard to believe it. Here were Tom and I – I'd turned twenty only just the other week – employing and giving orders to a team of staff. The most surprising thing about this – it must strike everyone who gives instructions to their own staff for the first time in their life – was this: they did what they were told!

Very late on we managed a quick nightcap with my parents. We telephoned John and Hannah, still in Wye for the present. They'd be coming up next week. Kyle and David had had dinner in the restaurant that first night. They left us to it afterwards, but said how wonderful the food was, and congratulated both of us, and said see you tomorrow, before they went.

And then we went to bed.

We stood in the bedroom together, facing each other, fully clothed. Then Tom reached out towards me, took my tie in his fingers, and undid it for me with great care and tenderness. I did the same for him.

It seemed a long time since we'd done this. And this time, because we were both dressed quite formally, there were a few more clothes to deal with. But eventually we stood together, revealed in our shared nakedness. Tired to the point of exhaustion Tom might be, but he still looked lovely, fresh as a daisy, and his cock was jauntily erect. Then he spoke, and it was as if he'd read my thoughts and was now reading them aloud, back to me, although he was speaking for himself.

'You're looking lovely, Mickey,' he said quietly. 'And you've done an amazing job of work today. I'm not surprised your cock's looking proud of you. It has every right to be – just as you've every right to be proud of it. And I'm proud of you, of course.' He reached an arm around my neck and pulled me towards him like a winch. 'Now come to bed.'

We climbed in together, and wrapped our legs around each other, allowing our cocks to fence for a while, unsure for the moment what exactly we were going to do with them that night, or if we were too tired, perhaps to do anything at all. In which case, it hardly mattered. This wasn't the last day of our life together. It felt in a way like the first, and that all the rest were still ahead of us, still to come. Each one an unexplored new wonderful country, waiting to be visited and inhabited by us.

THE END

####

Sweet Nineteen is the first in Anthony McDonald's series of twelve Gay Romance novels. A full list of these, and of other Anthony McDonald titles, appears overleaf.

Anthony McDonald studied modern history at Durham University, then worked briefly as a musical instrument maker and as a farmhand before moving into the theatre, where he has worked in every capacity except director and electrician. He has also spent several years teaching English in Paris and London. He now lives in rural East Sussex.

Novels by Anthony McDonald

Gay Romance Series:

Sweet Nineteen
Gay Romance on Garda
Gay Romance in Majorca
Cocker and I
Cam Cox
Gay Tartan
Tibidabo
The Paris Novel
The Van Gogh Window
Romance on the Orient Express
Spring Sonata
Touching Fifty

Also:

ADAM
BLUE SKY ADAM
GETTING ORLANDO
ORANGE BITTER, ORANGE SWEET
ALONG THE STARS
WOODCOCK FLIGHT
THE DOG IN THE CHAPEL

Anthony McDonald

TOM &CHRISTOPHER AND THEIR KIND
DOG ROSES
SILVER CTY
RAPH: DIARY OF A GAY TEEN
THE RAVEN AND THE JACKDAW
MATCHES IN THE DARK:
13 Tales of Gay Men
(Short story collection)

All titles are available as Kindle ebooks and as
paperbacks from Amazon.

www.anthonymcdonald.co.uk

Made in the USA
Las Vegas, NV
30 May 2022